ANIMAS FORKS

ALSO BY B.N. RUNDELL

Rindin' Lonesome

Star Dancer

The Christmas Bear

Buckskin Chronicles

McCain Chronicles

Plainsman Western Series

Rocky Mountain Saint Series

Stonecroft Saga

The Quest Chronicles

ANIMAS FORKS

A QUEST CHRONICLES NOVEL
BOOK 8

B.N. RUNDELL

Animas Forks

Kindle Edition

Wolfpack Publishing
1707 E. Diana Street
Tampa, FL 33610

www.wolfpackpublishing.com

Editing by My Brother's Editor

Paperback ISBN 979-8-89567-583-0
Ebook ISBN 979-8-89567-582-3

ANIMAS FORKS

1

HIGH COUNTRY

THE SPLASH OF MOLTEN GOLD POURED OUT BY THE SETTING sun was almost blinding as Cord sat, leaning forward on the pommel of his saddle, enjoying the beauty of the high country. The blanket of white-barked and gold-leaved aspen lay warm across the laps of the big mountains, while legions of stiff-legged lodgepole pine standing tall like soldiers arrayed in their dark cloaks, marched up the steeper slopes toward the naked peaks that stood proudly high, keeping watch over the natural beauty of the Rocky Mountains. The bottoms of the draws were painted in shades of deep red and orange as the leaves of the sumac, scrub oak, maple, and chokecherry became the palette of colors in shades of red for the Creator. This was a sight that never tired Cordell Beckett, the magnificence of the unrivaled masterpiece was what he often reveled in, and the fall was his favorite time.

He needed this time alone, having spent several

days at the negotiating table with Chief Ouray of the Tabeguache Ute and the many Indian agents, Washington Commissioners, and Felix R. Brunot, the chairman of the Board of Indian Commissioners. It had been an exhausting time at the Los Piños agency and he had gone only at the plea of Chief Ouray, his longtime friend. But now the preliminary agreement was hashed out and he could no longer involve himself, so he had chosen to take some solitary time in the high country of the Colorado territory and the Rocky Mountains.

He knew he had little time to make his camp, and he stood tall in his stirrups, looking across the long valley, focusing on the tree lines near the water. He needed grass for his horse, the long-legged grulla stallion he called Kwitcher, and the ever-present pack mule known only as Mule. His faithful hound, Blue, stood nearby, tongue lolling, as he too watched the setting sun. Cord dropped into the seat of his saddle, nudged Kwitcher toward the edge of the aspen, hopeful of making his camp before the melting sun caught the edge of dusk's curtain and lowered it behind the tall San Juan mountains.

Cord was a tall, broad-shouldered, and clean-shaven man, confident in his position of deputy U. S. Marshal whose territory was the third district of Colorado Territory. The district covered most of the southwest quarter of the territory and encompassed the land of the Ute people and the most recent gold strikes that drew prospectors and other gold hunters into this country. And with all these happenings, the Ute being moved away to their promised reservation lands and the influx of money-hungry miners and land-hungry settlers, Cord had more than his share of lawbreakers.

He wore a Colt .44-40 holstered on his left hip, butt forward, having surrendered his Remington Army .44 to the role of back-up in favor of the newer model Colt. He also carried that second pistol in his saddlebags. A scabbard under his right leg carried a Winchester Model 1873 in the same caliber as his pistols. The scabbard under his left leg carried a Spencer .56 with a telescopic sight for his long-distance shooting. Behind his neck, hanging between his shoulder blades under his shirt was a scabbarded razor-sharp Bowie knife. Aboard the pack mule was a Greener 12-gauge coach gun, and of course, ample ammunition for all his weapons. And most would consider his skill as a fighter to be his most formidable weapon, having had considerable training as a young man from his father. His father had fought with the British during the Battle of Pinjarra and had received an officer's commission. He also fought with the Ottoman Empire as an officer during the revolt in Tripolitania. Although his father would never talk about his wartime exploits, he shared with Cord the many ways of fighting he learned. What had suited Cord the best was the hand-to-hand combat or what would become known as martial arts. What he learned from his father was a unique blend of Muay Thai, from Thailand, and Capoeira from enslaved Africans in colonial Brazil, with elements of jiu-jitsu. But Cord had developed his own style using moves from all those taught by his father, for his father always said, "You have to use what is natural and comfortable for you, not what works for others. Sometime you may have to defend your life, or the lives of others and you won't have a weapon other than your own body."

Below him wound the Rio Grande River, making its way through the valley of the San Juan Mountains, the valley bottom showing tall grasses and several miners' prospect holes scarring the hillsides. But the colors of the golden aspen would not be dimmed by fading dreams of gold hunters, and Cord nudged Kwitcher into the edge of the trees for enough of a clearing by the little spring-fed stream to make a comfortable camp. He was downstream from the little settlement called Willow, a place where silver had recently been discovered, and several miners were digging for the precious metal, but most were looking for gold.

This was familiar territory for Cord. He had scouted it out shortly after he had been appointed the district deputy, a little over three years ago. Because of his duties, he had become all too familiar with the country, and the people had also become well acquainted with the no- nonsense marshal. His reputation had grown and he was well respected by most in the district. Now, after his long negotiations at the treaty table, he just wanted some free time. He had built himself a comfortable cabin near Wagon Wheel Gap but had spent little time there, his duties keeping him on the move. He was hesitant to return there, knowing there would probably be more than enough registered complaints and reports of outlawry, to keep him busy for some time. His contact point was with the general store owner in Wagon Wheel Gap, a fella called Toots Monroe, who had become a good and reliable friend. But the nearest jail was in Saguache, where the local county sheriff, a new man named Ira Dyar, kept his office near the Saguache County courthouse.

Before going to the treaty negotiations, Cord had dropped off a couple prisoners at the county jail to await the traveling judge, District Court Judge James Belford. He would often have to wait for the trial proceedings, but on occasion, he would leave the prisoner and the evidence with the sheriff, asking him to send one of those 'new-fangled-telegrams' to Wagon Wheel Gap to tell of the judge's expected appearance. But Cord did his best to dispel those thoughts from his mind for now, he just needed some time to relax and refresh a mite, maybe even do a little fishing and catch some nice trout for his dinner.

With his horse and mule stripped, rubbed down, and picketed, Cord grabbed his fishing gear and headed down to the bend in the river that he was certain was calling his name. There would be about an hour of fading light left to try his hand, and he was anxious for the distraction. He had learned a few things from his friends with the Ute people, some tricks from other friends, and now he was anxious to apply his own skills to the task. He had recently received a gift of a Samuel Phillipe cane fly-fishing rod from a man who had a problem with a claim jumper and Cord had helped save his claim and his gold. The man took his fortune and returned to Pennsylvania but had sent Cord the fly rod as a gift of appreciation. They had talked about fishing while they were together awaiting trial for the claim-jumper, and Cord had expressed his desire to one day spend more time enjoying the leisure activity, never thinking he would be rewarded in this manner.

With his rod in one hand, a small leather wallet with artificial flies in the other, he slowly approached the backwater at the bend, anticipating the evening feeding trout to begin jumping for the late season feast. Standing back from the edge of the grassy bank, Cord began his cast, the same way he had been practicing, and soon dropped the deer hair fly on the water. It had no sooner touched the surface, and a big cutthroat native trout splashed the surface, showed his shiny scales, flipped his tail, and dove for deep water. Cord grinned, hauled back on the line, lifting the tip of his rod, and the fight was on. The big trout ran deep, quickly rose to the surface, and tried to shake the hook free, but splashed down, and fought against the force of the line. Cord enjoyed the battle, pulling, cranking his reel, lifting the rod, all while doing everything as delicately as possible to prevent jerking the hook free, and within moments, the tired fish jumped from the water and Cord dropped him on the grass, still flopping with his shiny scales reflecting the last of the day's light.

After removing the hook, checking the line, and stepping back, Cord repeated the action and soon landed two more cutthroat native trout, each one about fifteen inches long and heavy. With the prizes on a willow fork stick, he walked back to his camp, watching the last light of day slip away under the lowering curtain of dusk. When he came to his camp, the horse and mule were standing, heads high, but not looking at him. Instead, they were looking upstream at the tree line where two riders were moving his direction. Cord dropped the fish near what would be his fire, snatched up his Winchester, and stood quietly, watching the men. He did not think they had seen him, he had walked to and from the river in a dry creek bed and was not immediately visible, but he could not be certain. Now he was surrounded by aspen and pine that offered a mottled hideaway and he leaned against the trunk of a tall ponderosa whose drooping boughs added additional cover.

As the two riders passed, Cord squinted to see them and noted they did not appear to be the usual prospector type looking for gold but rather had what he thought was an outlaw look about them. They showed holstered sidearms, rifles in scabbards, bedrolls, and saddlebags, but no sign of any prospecting gear and no pack animals behind them. These were the kind of men whose only tools of their trade were worn in holsters or carried in scabbards and a close inspection would probably show hands without callouses.

It was already too dark to get a good look at the men, nor were they close enough to hear any conversation. They were moving south alongside the river, keeping to the wagon road, unconcerned about any trouble, which usually meant they were bringing their own trouble. Cord frowned, shook his head, and watched as they moved out of sight. The only settlements downstream were Wagon Wheel Gap and further down at the mouth of the valley was the Mexican settlement of La Loma. With a last glance at the two riders, Cord returned to his camp and began making his fire to fry up his fish for supper.

2

RECON

THE GREY LIGHT OF EARLY MORNING WAS JUST BEGINNING to show in the eastern sky. The skirt of darkness was slightly ruffled as the dark-bellied clouds hindered any hint of light and the lanterns of the sky were snuffing out their lights. Cord slowly opened his eyes, just a slit, and without moving, he took stock of the sounds and movements of his camp. Satisfied all seemed to be well, he turned his head just enough to look around for a quick survey of his camp. He slowly rose, rifle in hand, and came to his feet. With another glance around, he picked up his Bible, and started uphill through the trees to go to the promontory he spotted yesterday before making his camp. It was a shoulder of rock that protruded from the trees, offering him a secluded spot that still afforded a good view of the valley and the surrounding countryside.

As the sun began to announce its coming with

brilliant splashes of gold on the bellies of the low-lying clouds, the bright colors reflected onto the treetops and rolling hillsides, giving the valley a muted glow of color that began to change into shades of pink slowly to the sleepy colors of early morning. Cord watched the colors dance across the horizon, accenting the dark silhouettes of the mountains, and laying the thin veil of color down into the valley. He lifted his eyes heavenward and began to thank his God for the gift of another day and the very breath of life.

He turned his attention to the open Bible in his lap and his eyes fell on the last verse of Isaiah 40, verse 31, *"But they that wait upon the Lord shall renew their strength; they shall mount up with wings as eagles; they shall run, and not be weary; and they shall walk and not faint."* He took a deep breath of the clear mountain air and lifted his eyes heavenward and felt as if God had spoken directly to him for this day and Cord was startled by the high-pitched scream of a circling bald eagle that drifted on the updraft of the mountain valley, his head down, wings wide, as he searched for his daily bounty. The cry of the bold raptor brought a smile to Cord's face as he whispered, "Thanks God."

Cord rose from his seat, took a lingering look up and down the wide, long valley, saw nothing amiss and started back to his camp. He thought he would have a leisurely day and a good breakfast. In little time his fire was crackling, bacon sizzling in the pan and biscuits baking in the small Dutch oven. A hail from below startled him and he came to his feet, rifle in hand. A quick look through the shimmering aspen showed a lone rider on a big blaze-faced bay horse, trailing a heavily loaded pack mule. A whiskery-faced man stood in his stirrups, waving his wrinkled hat over a grinning face as he called, "Hello the camp! I'm frien'ly an' hongry! Can I come in?"

Cord chuckled, answered, "Come ahead on, but keep your hands empty!"

"Hah! Muh hands'll be as empty as muh belly! Hehehehe..."

The man started to get down, but pulled a strap beside the pommel and an extra stirrup tumbled down below the usual stirrup and with another cackle as he looked at Cord's scowl, he said, "I'm so short I gots to have two stirrups to reach the ground! But it ain't so much the gittin' down as it's the gittin back up!" As he spoke, he bellied down on the seat of the saddle, slid down the length of the stirrup fender, stuck one foot in the higher stirrup, and used the second stirrup for his other foot, then stepped to the ground. He turned around to face Cord, a wide grin splitting his whiskers as he stuck thumbs behind his galluses and said, "Here I be! Now, how's 'bout lettin' me help with that thar breakfast—that is if'n you gonna share it?!"

Cord chuckled and nodded to the Dutch oven that sat under simmering coals, "You can check on the biscuits while I finish the bacon." His visitor was shorter than most, standing a bit shy of five feet, but made up for his lack of height by his breadth. His hair and whiskers were mostly white with a touch of red and the man reminded Cord of descriptions of Santa Claus as a "right jolly old elf!"

The happy man grinned widely and answered, "I can do that, an if'n you like eggs, I gots me a hand full fresh duck eggs in muh pack yonder!"

"Sure! Fetch 'em an' I'll cook 'em!" replied Cord, dropping to one knee by the fire as he took hold of the glove-wrapped skillet handle.

Breakfast was mostly a silent affair with all attention given to the devouring of the fare, but they soon leaned back, and Cord refilled their tin cups with hot coffee. The visitor held the steaming cup with both hands and looked over the rim at Cord, "They call me Whiskers, you?"

"I usually answer to Cord, or Marshal," he answered, grinning as he took a lingering sip, watching the man's reaction.

"So, that's what that thar shiny thing is you got pinned to yore vest! Whatchu marshal of?"

"Third district, Colorado territory. That's this southeast quarter of the territory."

"Ain't never heered o' you. That good, or bad?'

"That you've never heard of me? Dunno, reckon it could be either—good or bad, depends on the comp'ny you been keepin'." Cord grinned and chuckled as he looked over the rim of his cup at Whiskers.

"Ain't been keepin' no comp'ny...ain't safe nowadays!" grumbled Whiskers. He sipped his brew, staring into the glowing embers. "Keep to muhself mostly. Can't find nobody to trust—even wonder 'bout muh own self sometimes! Hehehehe...that's why I grew these whiskers! I threw away muh mirror cuz that fella that was lookin' back at me? Din't look too trustworthy, nohow! So...I up an' throwed him away too! hehehehe..."

"So, you givin' up on the gold hunt, are ya'?" asked Cord as he began the cleanup and preparing to pack up and head out.

"You might say that..." drawled Whiskers, rising to his feet to help with the clean-up. "Say, youngster, where 'bouts you headed from hyar? Cuz, if'n yore headed downstream, I'd admire to ride wit'cha. I'd like the com'ny and yore a purty good cook! Wal, good anyways, don' know 'bout the purty! Hehehe!"

Cord glanced at Whiskers over the back of the mule as he packed away the Dutch oven and frying pan. He answered, "Hadn't made up my mind, but I s'pose I could go downstream a ways. Got a cabin down by Wagon Wheel Gap, and I could make a visit to Saguache."

"They got 'em a stage stop o'er to Saguache yet?"

"Yeah, and a telegraph, and a freighter and a few other stores an' such. Got sumpin' special in mind?" asked Cord.

Cord chuckled to himself as he watched the short-legged Whiskers waddle over to his horse and using the double stirrup contraption, climb aboard his mount like a man climbing a ladder. Once seated, Whiskers laughed, waved at Cord, "Lead off, muh newfound friend, lead off!"

The sun was to their backs as they moved from the trees and took the trail across the plateau that skirted the high mountains behind them. Cord noticed the gathering clouds that sought to hide the morning sun and felt the cold air of winter's breath curl around his neck and probe at his shirttail. Across the valley, the gold of aspen painted the draws of black timbered mountains and splashed across the faces of the foothills. The trail dropped off the broad-shouldered mesa and joined the fledgling freighter road that sided the Rio Grande.

Cord glanced back at the clouds and said, "I think we're gonna be in for a snowstorm! But we should make the gap 'fore it comes!"

"Din't you say you had a cabin oe'r there?" queried Whiskers.

"Yup!"

And the snow came. Big tumbling flakes, driven by the wind, bouncing and dancing before the cold breeze, swirling under the hat brims, melting at the collars, and dusting the trail before them. Although it was less than ten miles to his cabin, Cord lifted his scarf around his face, hunkered his shoulders and ducked his head as the long-legged grulla and the pack mule following, quickened their pace. Cord knew the animals recognized where they were bound, and were as anxious as they to find shelter and warmth. He turned to look back at Whiskers and saw the little man perched atop his big bay horse and rolled almost into a snowball. White flakes decorated his hair and beard, clung to his woolen coat and scarf, and decorated the rump of the bay horse and the packs of his mule. The storm had blown up suddenly but showed no will to lessen anytime soon. Cord knew the early storms of the mountains were unpredictable at the least and deadly at best.

The muffled whistle of the storm soon turned into the howl of a lonesome wolf as the winds carried the snow down the canyon and deposited the flakes on the hillsides. Already the shoulders of the foothills were showing white, and the howl of the storm made the riders hunker into their coats, collars raised, scarves covering their faces, hats jammed down tight on their heads. With eyes slit, Cord thought he saw the rocky shoulders of the buttes that stood sentinel on either side of Spring Gulch. The crashing of water over the rocks of the riverbed told of the nearness of the Rio Grande and Kwitcher quickened his pace, recognizing the gateway to their gulch and their home.

Splashing across the water to reach the east bank, the animals made short work of the crossing. Fortunately at this time of year, the river flow was low and the crossing easy. Once into the gulch, the wind was abated by the tall shoulders and the rimrock cliffs. Cord let Kwitcher have his head and the big grulla again quickened his pace. A half mile into the gulch and the trail cut to the right to take to the trees and they welcomed the respite from the howling winds. They soon broke into the open, crossed a bit of a mountain meadow, now white with snow, and again entered the trees. The trail was familiar and they rode the shoulder of the hill before breaking into the clearing that held the cabin and corrals and shed. Kwitcher stopped at the corral gate, bent his head around to tell Cord to get off, and once free of his rider, the big horse shook free the snow in his mane and on his rump.

The men soon had the animals de-rigged and unsaddled and after rubbing them down, let them loose in the corral to find their own way to the sheltering shed and the grass hay that had filled the haymow. Cord and Whiskers carried their gear into the cabin and once inside, dropped everything and quickly set about starting a fire. With the blaze going and the heat filling the cabin, they both stripped off their coats and took a seat before the fire, hands held out to absorb the heat.

3

DIRECTION

CORD LOOKED AT WHISKERS AND ASKED, "UH, I NOTICED you had some heavy packs there. When you dropped 'em, I thought you were gonna break the boards on my floor. What'chu packin' anyway, rocks?"

"Ah, ain't nuthin' much. But I jus' don' like throwin' things away, you know how 'tis, 'bout the time you throw sumpin' away, you have a need for it. So..." he shrugged, grinning as he stretched out his hands to the fire.

Cord knew exactly what he meant; his mother had been like that. He fondly remembered times when his father chided his mother for never throwing anything away, only to hear her usual response, "Well, you just never know when we might need something like that again, and I just can't make myself throw away something that still has some usin' left in it!"

Although Cord suspicioned that Whiskers was

packing something special, it did not really concern him and he knew Whiskers had every right to his gear and secrets, if there were any. Cord rose, glanced at the old sourdough and said, "I'm turnin' in. You can roll out'chur gear right there in front of the fire, if you're of a mind to, but I'm goin' to my bed back yonder," nodding to the other room that held his bed and other gear. With a nod of his head, he moved away from the firelight and heard the rustling of the old-timer as he rolled out his bedroll. Blue padded behind Cord and they both turned in for the night.

Cord, usually an early riser, was surprised to smell coffee and more as he rolled from his covers. A glance to the window showed just the beginning of light, more from the brightness of the snowfall than from the rising sun that had yet to show its face to the new day. He pulled on his boots and tucked in his shirttail, slipped the galluses over his shoulders and donned his vest. With his fingers running through his hair, he pushed open the door and was greeted with an overly cheerful, "Mornin' sunshine!" from the whiskery-faced man that resembled an elf from the North Pole more than a sourdough prospector. But the grin was contagious and Cord smiled as he answered, "Mornin'. Is that bacon I smell cookin'?"

"It is! An' I got some biscuits in the Dutch oven! Couldn't find much else, so, I reckon that'll hafta do for now!"

"That's mighty fine. Ain't had nobody cookin' for me...well, in a coon's age, I reckon."

"Don't git used to it! Ain't gonna be no habit, that's fer sure'n certain!" declared Whiskers, chuckling to himself.

Cord went to the door, pulled it open and stepped out on the stoop for a looksee at the morning. The white blanket gave the entire hillside and surrounding trees an entirely different look. Cord stretched, took a deep breath of the crisp morning air, his front door faced to the northwest and the long vista across the valley was marked by the series of rimrocked flat-topped mesas and the long line of silhouetted Sangre de Cristo mountains to the far west. He turned and glanced to the eastern sky to get an idea of the coming morning, but the bashful sun was still hidden behind the ridges and mountains of the San Juan range that proudly stood across the long valley of the Rio Grande. He turned back to the interior of the cabin, pulled the door shut and took a seat at the small table, watching Whiskers tend the bacon.

"You know, you might make some woman mighty happy with your gettin'up an' cookin' first thing in the mornin'!" he chuckled.

"Already got me one! She's waitin' for my return, an' I'm anxious to get returned! hehehe." As he chuckled, his belly bounced and he twisted around on his one knee, pulled the frying pan from the fire and scooped up the bacon to drop it in the two tin plates at the edge of the fire. He brought the plates to the table, returned for the Dutch oven and sat it on the table before seating himself. He grinned at Cord and said, "Well?"

"Well what?" asked Cord.

"Ain'tchu gonna pray 'bout it?"

"Oh, yeah..." stammered Cord as he dropped his eyes and bowed his head and gave a short prayer of thanksgiving to the Lord and looked up at a grinning Whiskers. He lifted his eyes to the grinning Whiskers, "You got'ny kids with that wife that's waitin' for you?"

"Din't 'fore I left, but..." he shrugged, grinning.

"Well, how long you been gone?" asked a smiling Cord as he put some bacon between the pieces of biscuit.

"Couple yars," chuckled Whiskers, chomping down on his bacon sandwich. "But she was gettin' a li'l plump 'fore I left, so..." he shrugged.

Cord shook his head, grinning, realizing that his newfound friend was habitually vague and that he was not about to tell any more than absolutely necessary, which was the way of folks in the west, especially in gold country. Any man that shared too much would be liable to lose too much because there are always those about that prefer to take rather than earn any riches they may secure.

Cord glanced to the window, saw the morning light beginning to brighten the day and rose from his seat, "Well, Whiskers, I'm goin' into town to get any messages there might be for me, and from there, well..." he shrugged, showing both palms at his side as he rolled his shoulders and grinned.

"I'll be right thar wit'chu. You goin' any further down the road?"

"Might, depends on what's waitin' in Wagon Wheel Gap. And...if the weather's any indication, I might need to make muh rounds 'fore it gets any worse! I am due for a ride around my circuit that I usually take goin' the other way, but it'll be different this time. I'll be headin' down the valley and past the confluence, then out into the flats. Maybe turn north to Saguache, if I have any court dates I need to make, or go south and over the mountains and out past the hot springs at Pagosa, then to Silverton and so on."

Whiskers looked at Cord, frowned, "You mean to say you gotta cover all that?"

Cord grinned, nodded, "Umhmm, that's right."

"Good thing you ain't got'chu a woman! She'd leave you quicker'n a rattlesnake can strike!" Whiskers shook his head and turned back to his cleanup. "Be ready innaminnit!"

The town, if it could be called that, had grown since Cord first came into this area. Where before there were just a couple prospector's cabins, now there was the general store owned by his longtime friend, Toots Monroe. A saloon that called itself a hotel because it had a back room with a half dozen bunks, a livery stable with a blacksmith, another saloon, and an assay office for the recording of claims and weighing of ore. Several more cabins were scattered about, but this was mostly a jumping-off place for the many prospectors that had flooded into the area after the news of a few gold strikes spread. Although none of those strikes were at the Gap, this served as a supply point for many and continued to thrive through the good news and the bad. Now there was talk of both stagecoach company coming in as well as a railroad getting near further downstream and in the San Luis Valley.

Cord was greeted with waves and hellos as he rode down the main street, the dusty road that split the businesses. He stopped at the general store, slapped reins and lead around the hitch rail and with a nod to Whiskers who had done the same, the two stepped up on the boardwalk and entered the building. Cord stopped, letting his eyes get used to the dim interior, and looked about, grinning and nodding as a voice called from behind a counter, "Howdy Marshal! Good to see you back! Got some messages for ya'!"

Cord chuckled at the familiar greeting from his friend, Toots, and as he walked to the counter, he pushed his hat back on his head and accepted the handful of written messages. He turned and leaned back against the edge of the counter and began to read as he heard Toots greet Whiskers, "What'chu need?"

Whiskers handed Toots a paper with his list of

needs and Toots nodded and answered, "I'll get'er ready for ya'!"

The trail and wagon road stayed on the west side of the Rio Grande as it made its way downstream south and southwest. The river, with newfound water from the recent snow, crashed over the shallows and rocks as it hurried on its way to the confluence with the south fork as it neared its breakout into the San Luis Valley. Cord and Whiskers kept to the road, riding mostly single file but occasionally allowed to ride side by side, and Whiskers was a talker. Mostly asking questions, rarely giving any details about himself or his plans, but curious about just about everything.

Cord chuckled and asked, "You know, Whiskers, with all these questions, I'm beginning to wonder if you've even been out of those mountains for several years!"

"Wal, I ain't! An' I ain't had much comp'ny neither, nohow. So, you cain't blame a fella for wantin' to catch up. By the way, one question I been hesitant to ask, what year is it, anyway?"

Cord reined up, turned to face the old timer, leaned on his pommel, and asked, "You mean to tell me you don't know what year it is?"

"Wouldna' asked ya' if'n I did, now, would I?"

Cord chuckled and shook his head, "What year was it when you came into these mountains?"

Whiskers frowned, glanced about as if looking for a clue, then faced Cord, "It were 1868! I knowed that cuz I turnt fifty yar' ol'!"

"So, you were born in 1818?" asked Cord, incredulously.

"Wal, ain'tchu a smartie! 'Course I was! Now... what year do it be?"

"1874," answered Cord.

"Nah, cain't be! I ain't been gone that long! Nosir, you're foolin' wit' me!"

"1874."

Whiskers shook his head, mumbling all the while, giving Cord a suspicious look as if Cord might be lying or fooling, then slapped his legs to his horse and took the lead, dragging his mule behind. He looked at the riverbank, saw a break in the trees, a slough beyond and turned back to Cord, pointed, "That all right, youngun'?"

Cord chuckled, nodded, and followed Whiskers into the clearing and they began to set up camp, all to the mumbling and grumbling of Whiskers who stomped about, shaking his head.

4

VALLEY

I'M TELLIN' YA—IT CAIN'T BE!" SPAT WHISKERS AS HE dumped an armload of wood beside the beginnings of a cookfire. He growled as he put hands on hips and scowled at Cord. "It just cain't!" He was fussing because when he asked what year it was, Cord responded with the date of 1874.

Cord chuckled, "Now Whiskers, what reason would I have for lyin' to you? It don't make no difference to me what year it is, or what year you think it is, it's just what it is! Understand?" answered Cord as he set about getting the cookfire started. Once the fire was going, Cord skewered the remaining portion of the deer loin and hung it over the fire to begin broiling. He looked at Whiskers, "You gonna make some more o' them good biscuits like you done before?" nodding to the waiting Dutch oven that sat on a flat top rock beside the fire.

With a few more grumbles and foot stomping,

Whiskers sat down, gathering the goods around him and began fashioning his biscuits and placing them carefully in the greased cast iron Dutch oven. He commented, “Them things are big and heavy, take up a lotta room, but they shore is handy when it comes to makin’ biscuits!” he chuckled as he worked.

Whiskers looked at Cord as the younger man turned the venison loin to cook evenly over the fire. With a nod of appreciation, Whiskers asked, “So, when’ju think we’ll get into Saguache?”

“Oh, dependin’ on the weather, but prob’ly ‘bout dark day after tomorrow.”

“An’ you say they got a stage that comes there?”

“Ummhmm. The stage company took that route as an extension of the Cañon City run, up o’er the Poncho Pass, then to Saguache an’ up to what they’re callin’ Lake City, then down to the valley of the Gunnison. They’re expectin’ to get some good business shippin’ gold an’ such. But they’re also talkin’ ‘bout puttin’ in a railroad, so...”

“Bah! Railroad’s just ruin ever’place they go! Them things stink, make a lotta noise, an’ when they go bust, they just leave scars all acrost the countryside!”

Cord chuckled at Whisker’s comments, then asked, “Is there anything you like?”

“Lemme tell you sumpin’ youngin’, when you start gettin’ frost in yore hair,” he growled as he ran his fingers through the thick white hair with a tint of red that covered his head, "then you'll begin to unnerstan' what I'm talkin' 'bout!"

Cord chuckled, asked, "Better finish up those biscuits, this meat'll be ready in a short while."

THE MORNING CAME bright and warm, the azure blue sky arching overhead, not a cloud showing anywhere, as the two men rode from their camp and resumed their journey downstream on the Rio Grande. The sun was just showing its face and bending long lances of gold across the valley, making deep shadows of the hillsides to the west, and chasing the darkness of the night from the east-facing slopes. The valley began to open wide, showing deep grasses, scattered farms and ranches, and nearer the water were the ever-present hopefuls panning for gold. Canvas shelters of dirty white dotting the riverbanks, hunkered over prospectors shaking pans and hoping for any sign of gold. A few had shaker boxes to give them a greater opportunity for color and those camps usually had two or more workers, one or two shoveling the silt and rock from the riverbank, the other rocking the 'cradle' of the shaker box, watching the water and silt wash over the ripples and hopefully leaving behind the expected riches.

Most of the buildings were adobe, built by the early settlers who had obtained a land grant while the area was still under the control of Mexico. But the treaty of Guadalupe-Hidalgo transferred the land to the United States, and the settlers remained, converting their lands to homesteads and continuing their efforts at farming and a few making a go of ranching and raising livestock, although most cattle were Criollo, a breed similar to but smaller than the Texas longhorn. But cattle of any kind were in demand by the settlers and especially by the prospectors who hungered for anything but wild game.

The two men passed the little settlement of La Loma that sat back against the mountains to the east. The valley opened wide before them, the river carelessly meandering across the flats, and wide grassy plains that lay sleepily on either side. It was a lush land, and the few homes were more farms than ranches and the tilled fields were small. Cord's thoughts were about the potential of this land for raising cattle, beef that was in demand in all the gold camps. As he let his eyes wander over the valley, he pictured himself with a cabin or home there, at the edge of the trees on that slight rise that would give him a view of the rich valley, covered with cattle, maybe the new breed that was the talk of many, hereford, they were called, with their white faces and red beefy bodies. He grinned at his daydream, chuckled, and brought himself back to the present.

The hills on the north retreated and the wide expanse of the dry San Luis Valley opened before them. Their road or trail bent to the north to ride in the shadows of the foothills and plateaus of the San Juans. The long line of snow-capped peaks of the Sangre de Cristo Mountains marched along the eastern edge of the valley, now showing as a distant boundary of the wilderness. The trail took them over the rise of a long talus slope and Cord reined up for a better look at the valley. As he twisted around in his saddle, he frowned at the southern end of the valley, or what he could see from his promontory. It looked like a big dust cloud hanging low beyond the foothills and over the path of the Rio Grande. He shrugged, thinking it could be anything from a sudden dust-storm to a big band of migrating natives or a flurry of wind that raised a bunch of dust devils that were whipping across the flats. That was several miles away and of no real concern to him.

He dropped back in his saddle and nudged Kwitcher to move along. Whiskers brought his horse alongside and looked at Cord, glanced to the sun that stood high in the clear sky and asked, "Say young'un, shoun't we be stoppin' soon fer some food'n coffee?"

Cord glanced at the whiskery face that was split by a grin that showed tobacco-stained teeth, what there were of them, and laughed, "Is that all you think about, Whiskers? Food?"

"Wal, 'course not. On occasion, I have been knowed to have much grander thoughts. You know, 'bout riches, muh wife, an' a life o' leisure wit' servants doin' all the work. You know, like fixin' the coffee and such!" hehehehe. As he laughed, his belly bounced, and his smile grew wider, and his eyes danced with an abundance of mischief.

Cord waved his hand around, "Well Whiskers, I don't see any wood for a cookfire. All there is is cactus. Let's see, there's some prickly pear, course we could eat some o' that, but it don't burn so well. Then there's come hedgehog, and lots of cholla. Now, sometimes the dead cholla has some sticks that'll burn, but...I dunno. Mebbe we better wait." He grinned as he looked at the crushed hopes of Whiskers showing in his eyes.

"You're plumb discouragin'. You ain't much of a partner, nohow!" grumbled Whiskers.

"Oh, so now we're partners?" asked Cord, trying to look serious as he leaned on the pommel of his saddle and turned to face Whiskers. Their horses were ambling along with a rocking gait that Cord thought would make it easy to fall asleep in the saddle.

"Wal, o'course, we're partners! We been together longer'n some marriages, so I reckon that makes us partners—but that's just in the travelin' an'eatin' an' such. I ain't no partner when it comes to you bein' a marshal and shootin' the town up—that's fer dern shootin'."

"So, does that mean we're partners when you make that big gold strike?"

"Hah! You ain't done no work fer that, youngun'! I don' share in yore work, you don' share in mine!"

"Oh, I see how it is...we're partners as long as I have supplies, like coffee an' such, but when I run out, that dissolves the partnership?"

"Durn tootin'! So, you best not run out!" growled Whiskers, doing his best to mask his grin and keep from laughing.

"Well, I heard there was a new trader at the little settlement they're calling La Garita, so maybe we'll stop there, see if there's anything we're missing, you know, like having enough coffee!?"

"Good idee, partner! La Garita? Never heard of it!"

"Since you've been hidin' out for the last five years, I'm surprised you've heard of anything! There's little villages, towns and such, springing up all over! 'Course, most of 'em are just for the gold hunters, and will probably fade away 'fore they have time to become a real town, but..." shrugged Cord.

5

LA GARITA

THERE WAS LITTLE EVIDENCE THAT THE FIRST SNOW OF winter had visited the San Luis Valley. With the usual dusty hills lazily basking in the bright sunshine, sage and mesquite brush showing the same colors of faded green, and the gramma grasses, now dusty brown, waving in the morning breeze, it was more of a typical summer day than the coming of fall. Yet in the distance before them, the humps of timbered foothills displayed shoulders of gold where both aspen and cottonwood were strutting their colors and the lower reaches showed hints of red and purple from the scrub oak and kinnikinnick.

As the two men neared the flats that held La Garita, Whiskers looked at Cord, "Thot you said there was a settlement here! I don' see nuthin' but them two buildin's, an' one of 'em ain't nuthin' more'n a false front an' a big canvas tent!"

"That's the general store. The other'ns a livery. Don't need much else, do ya?"

"Why fer shore an' certain! Ain't a town without a saloon! Hehehehe."

"The general store does both. Supplies, drinks, and food," replied a grinning Cord, knowing his answer would bring a smile to Whiskers.

"Wal, that's better! Now I can wet muh whistle!"

"Can you even whistle?" laughed Cord.

"Phhhhtttt, phhhtttt, nope. Reckon that's why I need to wet it! Hehehehe..." chuckled Whiskers.

As they neared the general store, Cord noted two horses tied at the hitchrail, both with the saddles and gear of a vaquero. The charro saddles had the tall, broad, round, and flat-topped horn and pommel on the wooden tree covered with rawhide and the leather rigging was carved and one had inlaid silver embellishments. This was not the gear of gold hunters, but of the working vaquero in Mexico, and that piqued Cord's interest.

Cord and Whiskers tied their animals to the hitchrail at the side of the store and both stepped up on the boardwalk to enter the store. Cord stepped inside, quickly stepping away from the bright light of the entry and lowered his eyes and shaded his face with the brim of his hat as he looked about. He spotted the vaqueros sitting at a table in the corner, near the door, but with their backs to the wall and facing the door. They appeared to be busy with a meal and drinks, but Cord knew they were looking at him and Whiskers. Cord nodded to Whiskers, motioning to the counter and a table nearby. "Let's take that table and I'll talk to the boss," grinning as he motioned to the woman standing behind the counter.

Cord came near the counter, nodded, "Mornin' Mabel. Where's Horace?"

"Where'dya think? Up the crick, lookin' fer paydirt. Which he ain't never gonna find!" she growled, shaking her head. The matronly woman was in a gingham dress with a bonnet hanging behind her neck, a big apron that covered her front, and she leaned on the counter as she looked at Cord. "What can I do ya fer, Marshal?"

"Well, Whiskers and I will have some food and coffee, then we'll give you a list for some supplies. That all right?"

"Sure, sure," she answered, as she turned away to go to the back of the store where her cookstove held the makings for the meal.

Cord took a seat opposite Whiskers so he could face the front door and the table with the vaqueros. "Food'l be out in a jiffy," explained Cord. "You got anything special you want for supplies?"

"Wal since that fella in Wagon Wheel Gap was a lil' light, reckon we could use some more coffee, beans, bacon, you know, the usual. Won't need much if'n I'm catchin' a stage in Saguache!" he drawled.

"Gonna catch a stage, are ya? Where 'bouts you

headed?" asked Cord, watching as Mabel brought two steaming tin plates loaded with beans, potatoes and a big hunk of meat. As she sat them down in front of the two, she nodded when Cord said, "Thank you, ma'am!" and Whiskers echoed his thanks.

As Mabel toddled off to the back kitchen, Whiskers nodded to Cord, bowed his head and listened as Cord said a brief prayer of thanks. They looked at one another and Whiskers said, "Why, I be goin' home, where'dya think I'd be goin'?"

"And where's home?"

"Wal, muh daddy had him a bit of a farm back in Kaintucky. Twarn't much, but he twarn't much of a farmer nohow. But we made do. By the time I was oh, nine or ten, ol' William Clark laid 'em out a townsite and began buildin' a town just north o' the home place, called it Paducah, after some injuns, Comanche, I think. But Pa, he thot' things was gettin' too settled an' he up and packed ever'thin' in a wagon, hooked up the mules an' headed west. But he was kilt in a fight with them same injuns, an' Ma, well, she'n me and couple other young'uns, hitched a ride back to the farm and moved back in the ol' house. When she took up with a trader fella, he din't want no young'uns like me aroun' so I lit out on muh own, come west. But..." he paused to take a couple bites, "Heard later that muh two brothers wore blue in the war and both were kilt. Dunno 'bout Ma, ain't ne'er heard, prob'ly dead by now." He took another big bite, looked at Cord, and continued, "Met me a good woman on her folks farm south of Kansas City. I worked for her pa for a while, then we got hitched, and after her pa grumbled a mite at supportin' us on his farm, I took off to the gold fields. She said she'd wait, so..." he grinned, taking another big bite of food and reaching for the biscuits.

Movement at the far table caught Cord's attention and he saw both vaqueros rising from the table and start his direction. Cord frowned, but one man spoke, "*Perdón señor,*" and Cord turned to face the man, nodding, and answered, "Yes?"

"Did the woman call you marshal? Are you a lawman?" he asked, his English quite accented.

"Yes, I'm Marshal Beckett. Federal deputy marshal of this part of Colorado Territory."

"I see. Good." He paused, motioned to the empty chair, and at Cord's nod, he seated himself. "I am Miguel Hernandez, this," motioning to his partner—"is Elivé Martinez. We are vaqueros for Señor Dawson. We are bringing a herd to this land to settle and to have beef for the miners and settlers."

"Oh, that's good. How soon are you bringing this herd?" asked Cord, frowning.

"We are scouting the trail now. They are behind us and will be here in the next few days."

"And where are you settling?"

Miguel looked out the window and nodded, then waved his hand, "In this vast land. Between the Rio Grande and these two creeks that come from the mountains here. Everyone here in looking for gold, we bring beef to trade for their gold!" he grinned broadly.

"Will all of you be settling here—making a home here?" asked Cord.

"Many of the vaqueros will stay with Señor Dawson, but there are others who want to look for gold also."

"And when you say many, how many?"

"We have *trienta,* how you say, thirty?" and at Cord's nod, he continued, "We have thirty vaqueros, a few others that cook, handle the remuda, and drive the wagons. But there are probably about *diez* that will go to the mountains to try their luck."

"Well, good luck with that. But you should also know, the Ute people are not too happy right now so you should warn your boss to be careful with the natives."

"Si señor." He rose to his feet, extended his hand and added, *"Gracias señor."*

Cord shook his hand, nodded, and watched as the two men left the storefront. Whiskers looked at Cord, glanced back to the vaqueros, and said, "You're not likin' what'chu just heard, are ya?"

"Sounds like trouble to me, but...everyone is entitled to his own way of doin' things, as long as they don't cause trouble, but..." he shrugged as he stood and walked to the counter where Mabel waited. She had already gathered the goods on their list and looked at Cord, "That'll be a dollar six-bits."

Cord chuckled, paid with two one-dollar coins

and watched as Whiskers gathered up the goods and headed for the door. Cord tipped his hat to the woman, “Thanks, Mabel. See ya’ next time!”

“Be careful, Cord, an’ keep yore head down, y’hear?” she smiled her matronly smile and watched as he left.

6

SAGUACHE

THE WAGON SAT ALONE, DEBRIS HAD BEEN SCATTERED about, and from the slight rise where Cord had reined up and looked at the distant wagon with his binoculars, it appeared there were two horses tied behind the wagon. Between the wagon and the slight shoulder of the long slope of dry land that came from the foothills, there was someone, maybe two, busy with something, but they were too far away for Cord to tell just what they were doing. He turned to Whiskers, "I dunno what's goin' on down there, but I'm guessin' someone's in trouble. I'm goin' down there. If you want, you can come along or wait up here with the pack animals till I give you the high sign."

Whiskers huffed, "If you goin', so am I. You might need another hand if'n there's more'n one makin' trouble!"

Cord grinned, nodded, and nudged Kwitcher off the shoulder and started at an easy walk toward the wagon. As they neared the wagon and the scattered debris, it was evident there had been trouble. Cord reined Kwitcher toward the two that were busy with a shovel and more. They appeared to be digging at the edge of a slight bluff, but they were too busy to notice the coming of the two riders. Cord reined up, lifted his free hand high and called out, "Hello there! All right if we come closer?"

Cord's call startled the two workers, both jumped and stepped back. One held a rifle across his chest, the other had a shovel. The two were young, Cord guessed about ten or twelve years old, give or take, and they looked like mirror images. The one with the rifle was a little taller, the other a little stockier, both were towheads and freckle-faced. The rifle holder said, "Who're you? What'chu want? Don't come no closer!" as he spoke, he moved the rifle to place the muzzle in line with Cord.

Cord said, "Hold on there! I'm Marshal Cordell Beckett, and this is my partner, Whiskers. What's goin' on? What happened here?"

At the word *marshal,* the two young men looked at one another and the rifle lowered as the one explained, "We're diggin' graves for our folks. Some outlaws hit the wagon while me'n Colby,"—nodding toward his brother—"were up in the hills, huntin'. We heard some shootin', came runnin' back, but we were too late. We saw two riders makin' dust goin' back toward Saguache, an' found our folks all shot up and dyin'." The young man choked up as he related the happenings but fought to maintain his composure.

Cord swung down, tossed the reins of Kwitcher and the mule to Whiskers and walked to the young men, held out his hand. "Here. Let me help with that."

With shovel in hand, Cord worked and talked to the two boys, "So," with a nod to the taller boy—"you're Colby,"—then turned to face the other—"and you're...?"

"I'm Cormick."

"You boys twins?"

"Nah, but we're only a year apart. Colby's older," answered Cormick.

"What'chu doin' out here? I mean, where were you heading, and why?" asked Cord.

"We had been up above Saguache. We had us a cabin and Pa and us done some pannin' for gold. Made some, an' Ma wanted to homestead, make a proper home, as she called it, so Pa said Okay and we packed up and were goin' to where there was s'posed to be better land and less people. But now, I dunno." He dropped his eyes and sat down on the pile of dirt next to his brother, both sitting with slumped shoulders and heads hanging.

"Could you tell me anything about the two

outlaws that hit the wagon?" asked Cord, stepping back from the hole and motioning to Whiskers to give him a hand with the bodies. The animals had been ground-hitched and were grazing on the little bit of grass that grew nearby. As the two men carried the bodies to the one grave, they carefully lay them beside one another. The boys had wrapped the bodies in blankets, and now watched, tears in their eyes.

Colby spoke up, "Only saw the backs of 'em, but one was on a strawberry roan, the other'n on a blood sorrel."

Cord looked at the boy, surprised at his awareness and knowledge concerning the coloring of horses. "That'll help. After we're done here, we'll get whatever you want to take with you, then we'll go into Saguache, and maybe get an idea what to do then."

THEY MADE short work of the burying, praying over the graves, and packing up the few things of the boys to take with them. As they worked, the rest of the story came out. The boys had taken both horses and the only rifle to go hunting, the family needed meat. But that left only an old pistol for their dad, but they did not think they needed one anyway. There had been a four-up team of mules also taken by the outlaws and Cord believed the description of the horses and finding two men selling mules should be enough to identify the men and hopefully put them in jail in Saguache.

It was late afternoon when they started for Saguache, but Cord guessed it to only be about ten miles, and they could make that before dark. The boys sided the men, Colby alongside Cord and Cormick beside Whiskers. Whiskers chuckled, grinned as he talked to the boy, “So, youngun’, when you was back in Missouri, you do any farmin’?”

“Some, you know, plowed some fields, planted corn an’ beans, but the drought wiped out the crops. That’s why Pa was eager to go west.”

“You like farmin’ do ya?”

“It’s all right. I like seein’ things grow, but I’d rather be in the woods, huntin’.”

Whiskers chuckled, “Know what’chu mean. I’m thataway too, but...now I’m headin’ back to muh woman an’ she’s likin’ bein’ on a farm. Dunno though, might hafta move her somewheres’ there ain’t so durned many people!” he spat, the cheek full of tobacco had overflowed and was leaving a streak in his whiskers. The old man wiped his face, spat out the plug of chew and looked at the boy, “Got’ny idee what’chu gonna do? I mean, now that you’n your brother are alone?”

“Hadn’t thought about it much. Them outlaws took what little money we had, so I reckon all we gots is the horses and rifle. We’ll hafta figger out sumpin’ though.”

“Mmmmhmmm, reckon so,” mulled Whiskers,

running his hand around his whiskers, squinting, and thinking. He glanced to Cord and the other boy, Colby, and back to Cormick.

"Yore brother the older o' you two?" asked Whiskers.

"Only by a year. He's twelve an' a half, I'm eleven an' a half," as usual, the extra half a year being important to the young people.

Whiskers had recognized that Cormick was the more talkative and apparently confident of the two, but he also knew the quiet ones were usually the most contemplative and stronger of will. Whiskers was reminded of his own youth and the brothers he grew up with, both lost in the war between the states. The little time he had with his wife, they had talked about having a family and what kind of future they might have, but the overbearing presence of her father always seemed to interfere in any dreams or plans they talked about. That was part of the reason he was so willing to go west. He had been dreaming about making his fortune and showing her father that he was a lot more of a man than he thought. He and his wife had written one another, but time and the mail service had kept their communication minimal. The last word he heard from home was that his father-in-law had taken ill and his wife was hopeful he could come home, but that was nigh onto a year ago. But he was confident his return would be everything he hoped. Now he was thinking seriously of adding a little bit more to the surprise of his return.

Saguache lay at the intersection of two main trails. One that continued north and crossed the foothills of the Sangre de Cristo Mountains via Poncho Pass into the valley of the Arkansas River. The other going over the Cochetopa hills and into the valley of the Gunnison. The road traveled by Cord and Whiskers had come from the south of the San Luis Valley and the land that had been annexed after the Mexican-American War of 1848 and was what would one day become the state of New Mexico. It lay on the old Spanish Trail and had become a supply point for both travelers and miners.

Saguache was a growing town and Cord had known it almost from its beginning when Otto Mears had been instrumental in its founding and growth. That was the main reason Cord made this sort of his home base, other than Wagon Wheel Gap, because of the district court and the county jail. He was a familiar figure in the town and when the four riders reined up in front of the livery, he was hailed by the blacksmith and liveryman, Blake Hutchins.

"Well, howdy, Marshal! Din't 'spect you back so soon. Got some prisoners there wit'chu?" the hefty smithy chuckled as he put his thumbs under the straps of his heavy canvas apron that showed the work of the man. "Kinda young, ain't they—must be some wild outlaws you had to tame!"

"Nope. Just some friends. We need to put up our horses. Got room?"

"Yessir. Allus got room for you, Marshal! Just put

'em in the empty stalls back yonder, and as usual, if'n you needs to, you can put the gear in the tack room!"

"Will do!" answered Cord as he nodded to the others and stepped down. He handed the reins of Kwitcher and the mule to Whiskers and stepped closer to the smithy. "Say, Blake, you have any newcomers in earlier, maybe with a team of four mules they wanted to sell?"

Blake frowned, "You know, I was a li'l suspicious of those two. Strange they was ridin' an' leadin' a team that had all the harness still on an' such. They said the wagon broke down an' they decided to stick aroun' a while. But they had nuthin' else! You know, like baggage, boxes, an' such. Musta been an empty wagon."

"They still around?"

"I think so, must be, they put their horses in the stalls back there an' it's too late to be ridin' out. Prob'ly o'er to the saloon or mebbe the hotel next to it. You know the one."

"Ummhmm, I do."

"Be careful, Marshal, they look like purty salty fellas! The big 'un, specially!"

"What'd they look like?" asked Cord, waiting for the others to finish with the horses.

"Wal, the big 'uns got him a heavy bearskin coat o'er his red longjohns, floppy brown hat with holes in it. The other'n, wal, scraggly whiskers, scar across one cheek, his eyes...wal, they don't look the same place. One of 'em points off to the side all the time, an' he's got a mouth full o' rotten teeth—stinks too!"

"Thanks Blake," answered Cord, as the others came alongside.

7

STAND-OFF

“HERE, THOT YOU MIGHT WANT THIS,” SAID WHISKERS AS he handed Cord the double-barreled Greener shotgun from his pack.

“Thanks. I’m thinkin’ those two are in the saloon, and that’s next to the café there, so how ‘bout you takin’ the youngsters to the café, get somethin’ to eat while I go to the saloon, see if I can find those two hooligans.”

“Shore you don’ want me to side’chu?” asked Whiskers.

“I think I can handle it, ‘sides, them younguns’ are lookin’ a mite peak’ed, prob’ly purty hungry. And I don’t rightly want ‘em seein’ this. If Colby knew what I was doin’ I reckon he’d prob’ly wanna join in the fracas, an’ I wouldn’t rightly blame him. It was their folks, after all.”

“Ummhmmm. I been wonderin’ ‘bout ‘em, you

know, what they're gonna do now, where they gonna go."

"Well," drawled Cord, looking sidelong at Whiskers, "mebbe you can talk to 'em, give 'em some guidance."

Whiskers frowned, huffed a little an' said, "Whadda I know 'bout young'uns? Ain't never had none!"

"Unless I miss my guess, you were young once and in about the same predicament, from what you tell me."

As Cord stepped through the door of the saloon, he moved to the side, the Greener cradled across his chest. He wanted his eyes to get accustomed to the darker interior and he wanted to spot the outlaws before they laid eyes on him. The big room was crowded with about ten tables and chairs, most with patrons seated, some playing poker, others just drinking and talking, but several noticed the newcomer beside the door and nudged their tablemates to look at the marshal. The constant din of talking, laughing, cards shuffling, seemed to quiet a little.

Standing at the long bar that stretched across the back of the room, were several men, most looking like miners, but a few were dressed like farmers or cowhands. Two men near the end were attired in business suits and both had turned when Cord entered.

Standing side by side in the center of the bar,

were two that fit the description given by the liveryman, Blake. The big man was on the right and looked more like a grizzly in his bear skin coat, while the skinny one shuffled about beside him, talking all the while. The bartender saw Cord slowly approaching and with a glance to the two outlaws, he stood aside and joined the two businessmen at the end of the bar.

Cord stepped closer, brought the Greener down and stood slightly sideways to the men, the Greener held across his middle aimed at the two outlaws. He had loosed his duster, letting it hang open and show his badge pinned on his leather vest. Cord called out in a loud voice, "You two woman killers! You in the bearskin coat—turn around and have your hands empty!" The big man twisted around, turning only his head and looked over his shoulder at Cord and his eyes dropped to the big double-barreled coach gun. Cord said, "This is a 12-gauge Greener, and it ain't too particular where the buckshot goes, so be careful as you turn—both of you!" Cord spoke loudly in a commanding voice and the entire tavern fell silent, but the others at the bar moved well aside from the two outlaws.

The skinny one turned slowly, his eyes twitching and glancing about, drool coming from his mouth as he nervously started to lift his hands, whining, "Don...don't shoot...I ain't done nuthin'."

"Shut up, you dimwit!" growled the bigger of the two. The big man slowly turned, kept his hands at his side, but the front of his coat was open and his gun belt showed with one holstered pistol and another tucked behind his belt at his middle. He snarled and glared through hate-filled eyes, "Whatchu want wit' us? We ain't done nuthin' but have us a peaceful drink!"

"You murdered a man and his wife—stole their team, brought it in here and sold them to the liveryman!"

"We found them mules just a wanderin' in the open out there! We din't see nobody!"

Cord watched the big man who was slowly moving his hand up from his side and Cord said, "I told you—don't move! What you didn't see were the two young'uns—the two boys of that couple who saw you. You were riding a strawberry roan and skinny there had him a blood sorrel. You took the team of mules from the wagon after you killed the couple!"

"Tweren't no kids thar! Honest!" whined the skinny one, looking from his partner to Cord. "Say, ain't'chu that Bible totin' marshal? You ain't s'posed to be shootin' innocent folks like us! Ain't'chu s'posed to be forgivin' and such like?"

Cord let a slow grin split his face, watched the snaky one on the left inching away from his partner, and the big man had turned away slightly, probably to hide the movement of his right hand as he brought it up closer to his pistol. Cord answered, "That's right, but it also says *Vengeance is mine, I will repay...*" he nodded to the shotgun, "this here's vengeance, so if you want to personally meet vengeance, have at it!" he growled.

As Cord guessed, the big man had grabbed at the pistol tucked behind his belt and turned just enough to try to bring it level with Cord, but Cord dropped the hammers on both barrels of the shotgun, loosing the load of buckshot. The big Greener bucked, blasted, and spat a heavy load of buckshot that centered on the middle of the big man. The skinny one screamed like a scared girl. Blood blossomed across the big man's front, his chest, his chin and face and all the way down below his belt buckle and splattered on his partner. The big man slammed against the bar. The impact rocked the bottles and glasses on the bar, and wide-eyed, the big man slid to the floor in a heap of hair and blood. The echo of the blast subsided and everyone was frozen in place, as Cord broke open the breach of the shotgun and quickly reloaded with two shells, his eyes dancing around the room. He snapped the breach closed and looked at the skinny one.

"And that same Bible tells us to bring sinners like you to Jesus." He slowly lifted the muzzle of the shotgun, "And it's my job to arrange the meeting! Are you ready to make a personal acquaintance? You want a meeting with Jesus?"

"No, nooo, no!" whined the skinny one who stood, wide-eyed with each eye looking in opposite directions, his mouth agape as he began to whimper.

He looked to the heap of trash on the floor before him and sniveled, "You kilt him! You kilt Willy. Ain't nobody done that afore. You kilt him..." he wailed, almost crying.

Cord looked at the man, waved the shotgun, "Let's go!"

"Where we goin'? You gonna kill me too?" he whined, hands still raised as he took a tenuous step.

"I'm takin' you to jail. Your partner already met the judge, now you're gonna meet another'n." Cord looked at the barkeep, nodded toward the body, "Go through his pockets. He should have a good amount of money and maybe some gold dust. It belongs to the boys that're next door with Whiskers. Keep it for 'em." The barkeep nodded and watched Cord take the lone outlaw out of the saloon.

Dusk was settling over the valley, and the people of Saguache were moving about, most going to their homes in town while others were taking to their wagons and horses to go to their homes on the farms or claims hereabout. Cord marched the outlaw down the boardwalk, crossed the road to the sheriff's office and pushed his way in, following his charge. The sheriff stood, frowning, saw Cord with the shotgun and looked at the outlaw. "Want me to lock this'n up?"

"Yeah, but search him first. I'll keep the shotgun on him while you do. Him and his partner killed a couple, robbed them, stole their mules, and left two boys alone. Whatever money he has goes to the boys.

They're over at the café eating now, I'll bring them over after."

"The judge's due any day now, so you won't have long to wait for a trial," explained sheriff Ira Dyer, as he frowned, wrinkling his nose at the smell of the outlaw, and went through his pockets removing his pistol, knife, and a pouch of gold and a handful of coin and bills.

The outlaw whined, "That money's mine!"

"Not no more it ain't," answered the sheriff.

"Thanks, Sheriff. You had supper yet?" queried Cord.

"Nope. Let me lock him up and we'll go to the café together, since you're buyin'!" The sheriff grinned, hustling the skinny outlaw, who they found out was named Pete Folsom, into the cell. The sheriff was chuckling when he returned, "Has he been whining all this time?"

"He was whining, sniveling, and even crying after I shot his partner," explained Cord. He dropped his eyes, lowered the shotgun, and said, "Let's get us somethin' to eat. Not sure if I can eat much after the mess I made o'er to the saloon, but...it's still worth a try."

8

GUIDANCE

"WAL, HOWDY PARTNER! I HEERD THE ROAR O' THAT THAR Greener a while ago, but nuthin' after that, so I figgered ever'thin' was all right, so me'n the boys just been finishin' up wit' th'eatin'! You'n the sheriff thar fixin' to put on the feedbag, are ye?" declared Whiskers as he leaned back in his chair, thumbs under his galluses and a broad grin painting his face.

Cord chuckled, "That's right." He looked at the two boys, nodded to the sheriff, "Fellas, this here is Sheriff Ira Dyer. Sheriff, this here is Colby and Cormick..." He frowned, looking from one boy to the other. "Say, I never did get your last name, what is it?"

Colby spoke up, but it was not much more than a whisper, "Thacker." It was obvious the boy was thinking about his mom and dad. He glanced from Cord to Whiskers and back. "What's gonna happen with us, Marshal?"

Cord sat down, glanced to the sheriff, "Well, Colby. I don't rightly know. I've been thinkin' about that and haven't come up with a good answer just yet. I haven't talked much with the sheriff here..." he turned to face the sheriff, "How 'bout it, Sheriff? Any ideas?"

The sheriff frowned, "Wal, there's lots o' folks movin' in, but I can't say as I know of any that could take on the two boys. Most are hardly makin' ends meet themselves. You know, settin' up a new home, farmin' an' whatever. I haven't had much of a chance to get acquainted with 'em all, but...I'll ask around."

They were interrupted by the woman that ran the café as she poured the coffee and looked at the sheriff, said, "Well, Sheriff? You gonna have the usual?" and at his nod, she looked at Cord, "An' what about'chu, Marshal?"

"I'll have whatever he's havin'," he answered, nodding to the sheriff. The woman nodded and turned away.

Whiskers leaned both arms on the table and looked from Cord to the sheriff, glanced at the boys and said, "I been thinkin' 'bout that too." He looked at the boys and began, "Say fellas, I'm gonna be catchin' a stage and headin' back to Missouri to muh missus. We ain't got no kids, and she'd sure like a couple boys. How 'bout it? You could help with the farm work, I'd get'cha some new horses an' duds, and such. We'd go huntin' in the woods fer meat, an' all that sort o' stuff. 'Course you might hafta go to school," he looked at the boys' frowns, and continued, "but o' course, school ain't all the time and you might meet a couple purty girls thar. Hehehe...what say? Think you'd like to have me as an uncle or..." he shrugged and his eyes danced with mischief and hope.

The boys looked at one another, back to Whiskers and Cormick asked, "School? Would we hafta go?"

"Wal, it'd do ye some good. Tarnation, I went through the fifth grade an' see how smart I am! An' I'd bet ol' marshal here an' the sheriff, I bet they went to school, din't you fellers?" he asked the two men, received nods and grins from both and looked back to the boys. "Sides, it ain't all year long. Why, in the summer we'd go fishin' an' huntin' and such like."

The boys grinned, squirmed in their seats and Colby asked, "We got any other choices?" as he looked from the marshal to the sheriff and back to Whiskers. "What about you, Marshal?"

"Well boys, as much as I'd like to have two fine sons like you fellas, I'm just not home long enough to do that. I'm always on the move and much of what I do is a mite dangerous. It just would not be a good place for you. Not safe enough," answered Cord, frowning.

"Can we think about it?" asked Cormick, looking from Whiskers to his brother, who was nodding his agreement about the thinking.

"Of course you can, boys," answered Whiskers, "An' while you stay here with the marshal, I got some bizness to attend to." He looked at the sheriff, "Sheriff, you got an assay office hereabouts?"

"We do. It's right next door to the new bank," he pointed across the street. "You have some ore samples you want him to look at?" asked the sheriff.

"Oh, just a little poke," he answered as he patted the bulge at his waist. He rose and looked at the boys, "Now, you behave an' I'll be back right quick!" He turned and walked jauntily from the café to make his way across the roadway to the assayer's office.

Whiskers pushed the door open and stepped into the small interior of the assay office. The assayer sat behind a counter, his partially bald head shining in the sunlight that came from the window behind him. He scowled as he looked up at Whiskers, "What'chu need?"

Whiskers pulled out his poke and plunked it on the small counter that separated the assayer from the rest of the office, and asked, "Can you give me an assay on this?"

The man frowned, glanced from the poke to Whiskers, stood and picked up the poke and took it to the table that held his scales. He poured out a sampling, pushed his finger through it and with a flat-bottomed spoon, placed the sample of dust on the scale. After adjusting the weights, he looked at the prospector, back to the dust, poured the rest of the dust on the scale and adjusted the scale. He leaned back, did a double-take at the numbers, turned to look at Whiskers, "That all you got?"

"Wal, no. But I wanna know what it's worth?"

"Then you'll need to give me some time. You can either come back or wait, but it'll take a while," grumbled the assayer. "First I weigh it, then add flux and melt it, then it forms a button, and I have to separate it from the waste and add acid, then you get the final weight."

"I'll just wait an' watch, if'n that suits you?"

"Of course," answered the assayer, already getting an idea of the value. He could tell by the weight of the dust that it was extra heavy and possibly held considerable gold. He busied himself with the process, often mumbling to himself and giving an occasional glance to Whiskers who stayed standing and leaning on the narrow counter, watching everything the man did in his work.

It was mid-afternoon when the assayer pushed his glasses up on his forehead and leaned over the counter with a piece of paper and the button of gold. He shook his head, mumbling to himself, and looked at the button and back to the paper and then to Whiskers. "Mister, that's the finest sample of gold I have ever assayed. You say you have some more of it?"

Whiskers nodded, looking wide-eyed and letting a grin split his face as he looked at the man and the button of gold he held before him. When the assayer said, "That's point nine five fine! That's almost pure gold! How much you got?"

"Oh, I got a little bit, but how do I go about gettin' it swapped out for money, you know, real money?" questioned Whiskers, frowning.

The assayer shook his head, "Well, if you got a couple more pokes like this'n, I can swap it out for you, but if you have more'n that, you'll hafta go to the bank. But I'd prob'ly hafta go there with you to tell 'em what it's worth."

"Wal, where do we weigh it, here or thar?" asked Whiskers.

The assayer turned and pointed to his scales that sat on the desk, "I've got scales here, but..."

Whiskers chuckled, "Ain't big'nuff."

"Then we'll hafta go to the bank. Where do you have it now?"

"Oh, not far. How's about I jest meet'chu at the bank. Say, in just a little bit?"

"Alright. I'll go over there now and talk to Mr. Whitcomb, he's the president of the bank and he's Mr. Chaffee's nephew, that's Mr. Chaffee of the First National Bank of Denver," stated the assayer, as if that was supposed to impress Whiskers.

Whiskers nodded, "Back in a jiffy!" and walked out the door.

Cord had been watching the assay office while he and the boys sat at the table, finishing their meal and talking about what they might do for a home, when he saw a jaunty Whiskers come bounding out of the assay office. Cord frowned, said to the boys, "Uh, we better go see what Whiskers is up to, come on, boys," as he rose to his feet and started to the door.

They followed Whiskers down the street, chuckling at the antics of the man as he seemed to be dancing down the boardwalk toward the livery. When he entered the livery, Cord and the boys were close behind and Cord called out, "Hey Whiskers! What'chu doin'?"

Whiskers stopped in his tracks, turned, and frowning, asked, "You follerin' me?"

"No, well, yeah, I saw you come from the assay office, and you didn't come into the café so..." he shrugged. "What'chu up to?"

"Oh, need to get muh stuff. I'm glad yore here, you can help me! It's kinda heavy, ya know. I'll get the mule, you go back to the tack room and uncover muh packs," directed Whiskers as he stepped to the stall of his mule.

9

DECISIONS

"WELL, MR. WHISKERS, IS IT?" ASKED THE RATHER PORTLY gentleman attired in his dark business suit with a checkered vest that strutted a gold watch chain across his ample front. "I'm Jeremiah Whitcomb, and Mr. Thompsett, the assayer, and I have weighed out your ore and he tells me it is consistent with the sample you provided, so...we're prepared to pay you the calculated amount according to Mr. Thompsett's figures." He paused, motioned for Whiskers to have a seat before his desk as he sat down at his desk and began to scratch out some figures on a piece of paper. Whiskers nodded to Cord to be seated beside him and they waited as the man did his calculations. He raised his eyebrows, wrinkling his forehead and looked carefully at his figures and looked at Whiskers, pushing the paper forward.

"Now," he began, pointing at the figures. "You

see here is the total weight of the ore, 237 pounds, and Mr. Thompsett said your sample weighed out at point nine five fine, or 95 percent fine. So, 237 times 95 equals 225.15 times 16 ounces per pound equals three thousand two point four. That's three thousand two point four ounces. Now take that times the current price of gold of $20.67 equals $74,461.61." The banker smiled broadly and took a deep breath that lifted his shoulders and he leaned his elbows on the desk as he looked at Whiskers. "Now, what is your full name, sir?" Holding a pen handy ready to write it out.

"Uh, muh full name? Wal, it's..." he began, stammered a little and looked at Cord then back to the banker, "It's Ebenezer McGillicutty," and he emphasized the name with a jerk of his chin as if he was putting a period at the end of the statement.

Cord coughed, looked sidelong at Whiskers, and chuckled, "No wonder you go by Whiskers!"

"So, what'chu need that fer?"

"To make out the bank draft in your name," stated the president, showing little tolerance.

"Then what? What do I do with it?"

"Why, you can cash it here, or some other bank, or..."

"How can I send it back to muh wife?" asked Whiskers, frowning.

"Well..." grinned the banker, "there is a new way of doing that. You tell us where you want to send it and we can do what they call a wire transfer to a bank in that location. And when you go there, you will have an account in your name with all the money in the account."

"Then let's do that...but I want some money now, need 'nuff to pay muh way back there," he grumbled.

"How much?" asked the banker.

"Oh," he glanced at Cord, back to the banker, "Make it five hunnert now, the rest in that..." waving his hand at the banker's papers to indicate the draft. He looked at Cord, "You know 'bout them whatchamacallit things fer sendin' the money?"

"Heard of 'em. I think it's safe enough. Safer'n carryin' that much, that's for sure," declared Cord.

Whiskers looked at the banker, "Will you he'p me wit' sendin' that thar transfer?"

"I can do that. Happy to oblige, and it works better that way, when we send it bank to bank. Now, what bank or town do you want it to go to?"

"Wal, the farm's a mite south of Kansas City, little place called Lee's Summit. I reckon that Kansas City's the biggest town thereabouts, so send it to a bank thar."

The two friends were quiet as they walked back to the sheriff's office where Ira Dyer had said he would be with the boys when they returned. Blue, Cord's faithful hound, trotted quietly beside them as Cord looked at Whiskers, "What'chu gonna do now?"

Whiskers chuckled, "You mean, now that I got all that money?"

Cord laughed, "Well, that too. But I was thinking about the boys. You still thinkin' about taking them with you?"

"Ummhmm, I think Eleanor would like to have 'em underfoot. We talked 'bout havin' young'uns, but..." he shrugged.

"Does she know you're coming home?" asked Cord.

Whiskers grumbled, "Hmmm, mebbe I oughta send her one o' them thar tellygrams, ya' reckon?"

"Seein' as how you'd probably get there before a letter, yeah."

Whiskers stopped, turned around and looked at Cord, "Well...?"

"Well what?"

"Well, c'mon and he'p me do it!"

Cord chuckled and walked with Whiskers back to the telegram office to get the missive sent on its way.

After sending the telegram, they went to the Barlow and Sanderson stage company office and bought tickets for Whiskers and the two boys for passage through Cañon City and on to Pueblo. They were assured by the ticket agent that the Denver and Rio Grande Railroad served Pueblo and they could get tickets from there to Kansas City and probably on to Lee's Summit.

With that settled, the two men walked back to

the sheriff's office and on their way, Whiskers asked, "You think I'm doin' the right thing?"

"Well, I don't see as how the boys have much choice in the matter. They're too young to be on their own, even with the little bit of money they have now. And you've got time to go with them to the livery, sell the horses and tack, and maybe even get them and you some fresh duds at the general store, or maybe after you get to Cañon City. I'm sure you want to make a good impression on your wife what with surprising her with two young'uns."

Whiskers mumbled, nodded, kept walking and Cord added, "I think you're doing a good thing. Those seem to be good boys and with your guidance, I think they'll grow to be fine men. And I think your wife's gonna be pleasantly surprised with your fortune too!" he chuckled.

Whiskers laughed at that, "I was a bit surprised too!"

With the boys in tow, the men went to the stables to tend to the horses and talk about selling and getting new horses after the trip. Colby was especially interested in the horses, "Can I get a Morgan? I hear they're good horses for workin' with cattle an' such."

"I dunno 'bout that, but I reckon we can find you just about anything that'll suit you!" answered Whiskers, pleased that the boys were looking forward to the new adventure and trip.

Cormick said, "I want me a dog, like Blue! And a new rifle, one o' them Winchesters like Cord has."

"Well, we can prob'ly do that. You'll need one for huntin'. I'll make you a deal, you get good grades in school and I'll let you pick it out—how's that? And as for a dog, well, we'll just hafta see what we can find after we get there, but, yeah, every boy needs a dog!" answered Whiskers, grinning and squirming on his seat as he straddled the top rail of the stall.

10

CHANGE

THEY STOPPED BY THE SHERIFF'S OFFICE BEFORE GOING FOR supper. Everyone was grinning as they came into the office of Ira Dyer and the sheriff looked up at his visitors, "Wal, looks like you'ns have got your problems all worked out, am I right?"

"Reckon so, Sheriff. We even stopped by the stage office an' got us some tickets on the stage tomorrow!" declared a grinning Whiskers.

"Well, that's good to hear. I was gettin' a little concerned and runnin' outta ideas for the boys there. So, you're takin' 'em back east with you?" asked the sheriff, nodding.

He looked at Cord and back to Whiskers and both men discerned the sheriff had something to cover with Cord.

Whiskers grinned, nodded slightly to Cord and the sheriff, then added, "That's right. We're gonna be like a real fam'ly!" chuckled Whiskers. He looked at

Cord and the boys, then said, “Say, I reckon we got some time to see ‘bout some new duds. What’say we go to the store while these hyar law officers talk business?”

Cord nodded to Whiskers, “I’ll catch up with you at the café. That be alright?”

“’Course it be, an’ we’re gettin’ so hungry, won’t be long now! Hehehehee. . .”

Whiskers grinned as he hustled the boys from the office, turning down the boardwalk to the general store.

The sheriff motioned Cord to the chair in front of the desk and seated himself. He leaned back, looked at Cord and began, “Had a couple fellas through here two days ago, right ‘fore you came into town. They came here apurpose, thinkin’ I might have some jurisdiction or sumpin’, but...they were none too happy when I said there weren’t nuthin’ I could do, but I tol’ ‘em ‘bout’chu, but they weren’t none too happy ‘bout that neither. So, anyway, their story is that that area up the Animas River, round ‘bout where the West Fork of the Animas and the North Fork of the Animas get together, they’ve been hittin’ some good gold, not the pannin’ kind, but the hard rock kind. There’s been some that are gettin’ some good quartz veins that are laced with color an’ folks been gettin’ purty excited!” he chuckled as he leaned back in his chair, grinning and putting his thumbs under his galluses.

Cord frowned, “What’s that got to do with me? I

ain't lookin' for gold, an' even if I was, that hard rock stuff is hard work!"

"Wal, they was talkin' 'bout lode mining techniques and what it costs an' several of 'em was plannin' on gettin' together and poolin' their money to get the equipment they need. Then along come some ol' boy, big 'un they say, calls himself Bull, and some o' his thugs, an' he said 'tweren't no use in 'em poolin' their money, cuz he was takin' over ever'thing! When they started buckin' their neck to that idee, he up an' shoots a couple o' the miners, laughed an' looked at the others an' asked, 'Any questions?' The rest o' them boys just scattered, but they have the rightful claims, filed with the miner's district and some even with the county, but as you know, La Plata County and the upper end of it have been arguin' 'bout things. Most look to that place they're callin' Bakers' Park as the center but..." he shrugged. Then continued, "but that fella called Bull, done kilt the fella with the district, took o'er the claim setup, an' said, 'All claims belong to me now!'"

Cord leaned forward closer to the edge of the sheriff's desk, "Did you get the names of the men that came in here? And if they're goin' back?"

The sheriff rummaged around in his desk drawer, mumbling all the while, and came up with a piece of paper, and began to read the names, "Walter Trumbull, Festus Whitson, Jerome Whittaker, and Amos Manning." He handed the paper to Cord, and added,

"Dunno if they're goin' back, but they was purty sure they had some good claims."

"Well, I knew things were a little too peaceful to last very long. After the Utes signed that treaty, things will be changing mighty fast. With the natives leavin' that kinda opens everything up for the miners an' such, so..." shrugged Cord as he rose from his seat. "Guess I need to be gettin' ready for a long ride. But first, I wanna see Whiskers an' the boys off on the stage, then I'll head west. If you hear from those men, have 'em come to the hotel, or leave word with you or the liveryman."

"Will do. I don't envy you none. Sounds like a lotta trouble, what with the bull o' the woods doin' whatever he pleases. If he gets away with things long enough, he could destroy any evidence there ever were any legally filed claims and he could take 'em over, then there'd be no stoppin' him!"

"You wanna swap badges? I'll stay here an' sit in your easy chair, and you can take the long ride that's got trouble waitin' at the end!"

"Nosireee! My momma din't raise no idjits!" he declared, shaking his head and grinning as Cord left the office.

THEY HAD breakfast in the café and quickly made their way to the stage office. Whiskers and the boys had a canvas tote bag with their few belongings and it was thrown into the boot at the back of the stagecoach.

The boys were excited about their first stage ride and were anxious to get aboard, but Whiskers stopped them with, "Hey, boys, reckon you oughta be sayin' goodbye to our good friend, Cord?"

"Oh yeah," answered Colby with a glance to his brother. Both boys stepped closer to Cord and offered their hands for a handshake, something Whiskers had told them young men should do, and with broad grins, they both said, "Thank you, Mr. Cord."

Cord grinned, "Well, if you're gonna be usin' the mister—you might oughta know my last name is Beckett. So it would be Mr. Beckett, but between friends, I prefer Cord," he declared as he stretched out his hand and shook with both boys. "Now, you take care of Whiskers for me, now, will you? After all, he's gettin' a little old for this long trip so you might keep a close eye on him!" he chuckled as he glanced to a squirming Whiskers.

Whiskers stepped close, and shook Cord's hand as he said, "Muh life is shore gonna be changin', what with young'uns around all the time."

"Oh, you'll be fine—they'll keep you young!" declared Cord. "And it would be good if you could drop a letter and let me know how things are going for all of you!"

"I'll do that! Might even have the young'uns practice writin' an' have them send one, ever' now'n then!"

Cord grinned, watched as they boarded and as the driver cracked the whip, the horses leaned into their traces and the coach rocked back on the thoroughbrace and they were on their way. Colby leaned out the window and waved, a broad grin of happiness painted on his face. Cord chuckled as he returned the wave and almost before the stage was out of sight, Cord led Kwitcher and the mule from the livery, and with Blue at his side, he too put Saguache behind.

Cord knew the trip to the forks of the Animas River would take at least a week, maybe more. At this time of year, snowstorms could blow up in a hurry and in the San Juan Mountains, they could drop several feet of snow in a day. He had been hopeful of staying near his cabin for this winter, but outlaws are not the most considerate of other folks' ways and expectations. And depending on how long it would take to get the issue resolved, he might be spending the winter in that area. He shook his head at the thought, knowing that was in the high country and the new diggings were all around timberline, which meant it was somewhere around 11,000 feet elevation. He shuddered at the thought of spending a winter around timberline, but...it wasn't up to him.

He was basically backtracking the route he and Whiskers had traveled, and he would at least have one night at his cabin, but before that he would have to spend a night or two on the trail. With the first night being at La Garita, then maybe Del Norte and if he made good time, he would be in Wagon Wheel

Gap for the third night and have the night at his cabin to get recouped.

He avoided La Garita by riding near the tree line and as dusk began to lower its curtain, he found a likely campsite near the little creek that came from the high country. He was well stocked on supplies and could forego a stop at the general store. He made camp in the gold aspen that sided the little creek and climbed the shoulders of the foothills. He enjoyed the constant whisper of the aspen as the slightest breeze made the flutter of the big golden leaves applaud the presence of the camper. After a quick meal of leftover biscuits and a strip of venison hung over the fire, he downed the last of the coffee and stretched out on his bedroll and let sleep take him away.

11

JOURNEY

After a night near La Garita, he pushed south toward Del Norte, and remembered his encounter with the vaqueros that told about driving a herd from the Santa Fe area and their plans to settle at the mouth of the canyon of Del Norte. He was no more than ten miles from La Garita when he saw the first of the herd. The cattle appeared to be mostly the Criollo that were common in Mexico, but others appeared to be the larger longhorn that were a derivative of the Criollo. The cattle were scattered about the flats that lay in the shadow of the foothills of the San Juan mountains, the foothills that already showed their brilliant colors of the gold of aspen and the muted reds of the scrub oak and more. The grass of the San Luis Valley was mostly the blue grama, but there were other grasses, wheatgrass, and Indian Ricegrass. The cattle would rove the land in their search for graze and water. But the farther they traveled for grass, the further they moved from water. And with winter coming on, staying near water would be primary, especially when the bitter cold of the mountainous country would freeze any standing and any slow-moving water. But there was always the hot springs, although those were usually too hot and contained too many minerals to make it very appealing to thirsty cattle.

Cord stepped down from his saddle, ground-hitched Kwitcher and the mule, and with Blue at his side, he walked to the point of the shoulder of land that boldly pushed out into the valley of the Rio Grande, forcing the river to bend around the shoulder to make its way further east and then to the south. Cord sat down, raised his knees and rested his elbows on his knees as he lifted the binoculars for a good look at the valley of the grand old river. The valley of the meandering river still showed green with the blue grama and other grasses abundant. The banks of the river were lined with cottonwoods, some shedding their rusty-looking leaves in the afternoon breezes, and the many oak, alder, and willows that crowded the bank pushing against one another for their fair share of the life-giving water and beginning to display shades of red.

The cattle moved lazily about, content with the lush lands, especially after their long journey from the south. As Cord scanned the valley, he spotted some activity to the east, on the flats but where the grasses were still thick, and he guessed it to be part of the homestead of the Señor Dawson talked about by the vaqueros. After he looked about some more, he decided to ride down to what he thought was the Dawson place and get acquainted.

John Barkley Dawson was well-known among cattlemen in Texas, New Mexico, Colorado and even into Wyoming and on to California. He had partnered with Charles Goodnight and Oliver Loving to take cattle to the gold fields in California in the two decades just past. Now he had brought a herd into the gold fields of the western slopes of the Rockies and had even grander plans for the future. He sat tall in his saddle as he looked at the many workers before him and leaned on his pommel, frowning. But his attention was caught when he saw a lone rider with a pack mule behind, approaching.

Cord raised an open hand high as he called out, “Alright if I come in?”

Dawson twisted in his seat to look directly at Cord, and with a nod, motioned Cord closer. The big man sported Van Dyke whiskers, a receding hairline, bushy brows, all of mostly grey. He was broad-shouldered, stern expression, and thick chest. Attired in the typical wool-lined canvas duster that showed the signs of the trail, his felt hat had been pushed back on his head to reveal the receding hairline. Wool britches were covered with buckskin shotgun chaps, and he leaned on the pommel to look at Cord with one eyebrow raised. "Who're you?" he asked, annoyance showing in his expression and his voice.

Cord grinned and nudged Kwitcher a little closer to the man. Cord extended his hand, "I'm Marshal Cordell Beckett and unless I miss my guess, you're the boss around here and that would make you John Dawson, am I right?"

The big man let a slow grin split his face as he extended his hand for the introductory handshake and answered, "That I am, and it's good to meet you, Marshal." He looked about, nodded toward a stump and log that lay near a small cookfire that had a coffee pot setting, at the foot of a tall spruce and said, "Let's light an' set a spell. I'd like to talk, if'n you've got the time?"

"Sure, glad to," answered Cord.

As they seated themselves, Dawson reached for the pot and a couple of tin cups nearby and began to pour the coffee. He offered the first cup to Cord who gratefully accepted with a "Thank you, sir," and took the first sip. Dawson sat back against the big spruce trunk, the cup in his hands as he looked at Cord.

"Well, I'm glad you came by, Marshal. Let me tell you about what's goin' on around here. We brought in around 4000 head of Criollo cattle to feed all the hungry miners and such. I learned a few years back that it's easier to bring in the cattle to feed 'em, than it is to try to dig out that stuff your own self. I've taken herds all the way out to California in the late '40's an' early '50's, up north an' aroun' Pike's Peak in the years gone by, an' now things are startin' to look good up here in the San Juan's an' elsewhere, so here we be!" he chuckled, taking another long draught of his steaming coffee. He shuffled around a bit to get a better seat and lifted his eyes to Cord, "And, as you can tell, I've got a crew of workers busy with building. They'll build a home, a barn, a stable, and maybe a bunkhouse. But they're good workers. I've kept them busy for some time now. They built our ranch house down south of Santa Fe on the Pecos and did a good job. So, I'm hoping they won't take too long on this," he nodded toward the men who were busy with shovels and more as they prepared the land for the home. "It's gonna be a Spanish-style hacienda, usin' the adobe from up there on the face o' that hill yonder," he nodded toward the hill where Cord had sat earlier as he looked over the valley.

"You see, I'll be getting married again right soon, and I'm not too sure where she's gonna want to live. I have a ranch down in New Mexico territory, and now this one here, but she's a widowed schoolteacher in Iowa and has not been any further west than Iowa."

"And after she makes her choice, are you going to keep both ranches working?"

"Yessir, however,..." he paused, took another sip of coffee, and looked over the edge of the cup at Cord, "My Segundo, Miguel Hernandez, the man I expected to stay hereabouts and keep the ranch going, has decided, along with several of the other vaqueros, to try his luck in the gold field, but at least he's passin' the word that we got beef for sale. So, for now, I'm not too sure exactly what will be happening."

"And if he's happy in the gold fields, what then?" asked Cord.

"Oh, if he don't come back, and if muh new bride don't want it..." he shook his head, grinning, "course I'm hopin' she likes this'n better'n the other'n. But..." he took a deep breath and another sip of coffee, "I reckon I'll just hafta find somebody else to run it, or, maybe even sell it. That, of course, depends on how the gold strike lasts and such, but, I'm always open for opportunities," he chuckled as he looked sidelong at Cord.

"But, unless I miss my guess, an' the way you've been lookin' at those beeves out yonder, you've had a hankerin' for the ranch life, ain'tchu?" grinned the older man.

Cord let a slow grin split his face and nodded as he looked back at Dawson. "Oh, you might say way back in my youth nigh onto the end of the war, my dad and I used to talk about the west and how we'd like to have a cattle ranch. But he was a preacher and I was just a boy..."

"Your dad was a preacher?"

"Ummhmm. But my family was killed by marauders, Red Legs, at the end of the war. Actually, the war was supposed to be over, but that didn't stop 'em," drawled Cord, scowling at the memory.

"That's too bad. But, interestingly enough, the

woman I'm gonna marry," and he grinned, dropped his eyes and his voice, "she'll be muh third wife, the first two both died, last one in childbirth. But she wrote an article in a Baptist magazine that I really liked, so I wrote to her and well, now we're gonna be gettin' married!" he declared, a wide grin showing his happiness.

"What was the article about?" asked Cord.

"Oh, it did a real fine job of explainin' how the Bible teaches about the need for anyone that wants to go to Heaven, must receive that free gift of salvation told about in Romans 10:9-13, and other places too, but she made it plain!"

"What about you, John, have you received that gift of salvation paid for by the blood of Christ that was shed on the cross for us?" *I John 1:7.*

"I have! And you?"

"Yessir, most certainly!" answered a grinning Cord, relieved to hear John's answer. Cord tossed out the dregs of his coffee and came to his feet. "I need to be going, John. It's been good to meet and talk with you," he explained as he extended his hand for another handshake.

"Likewise! And, say, do you get this way often?" asked John, also standing.

"Oh, ever' now and then, dependin' on what's happening and where. I was through here just a few days ago and met your Segundo and those with him. I was on my way to Saguache to help my friend and a couple orphan boys to get the stage east. But..." he shrugged as he moved closer to Kwitcher, "got a report of some lawbreakers up around the forks of the Animas, so I'm headin' up there to see if I can straighten things out a mite."

"Anything bad?" asked John as Cord swung aboard his horse.

Cord looked down at the man, "Oh, you know. Just somebody wantin' what somebody else has and tryin' to take it from 'em. The usual."

"Wal, whenever you're down thisaway, stop in. I'd admire to talk with you, get to know you better."

"I'll do that! And, if you're up Animas way, or any other place where things are goin' on, and I'm still around, you catch up with me and I'll buy you dinner!"

"Done!" declared John, as he stepped back and watched Cord ride to the riverbank and nudge Kwitcher to take the crossing. The main trail into the canyon of the Rio Grande was on the west side of the river and Cord needed to make time before dark.

12

JOURNEY

The darkness chased the tired Cord up the draw toward his cabin. It had been a long day, longer than planned, coming from the valley of the mouth of the Rio Grande and the new ranch of John Dawson. But during his ride, his mind took a journey back into his past. The story told by Dawson about his first two wives dying, and now he was going to be married again, reminded Cord of the women in his life. His first woman companion was Yellow Singing Bird, the Ute woman who had been captured by the Comanche and freed by Cord. She had attached herself to Cord even after he returned her to her people. Later, in the beginning of his hunt for the murderers of his family, the band of Red Legs, she was killed defending her man, Cord.

After that, he had found and married Tabitha Townsend. It was with Tabby that he expected to spend the rest of his life and raise a family, but he lost her in childbirth. After that, he focused all his attention on his duty as a marshal. But of course, there was the time with Lone Eagle, the woman shaman of the Ute who chose him during the Bear Dance. He chuckled at the memory and the time spent together. They had thought about more, but her duties as the Medicine Woman of her people and his duties as a marshal seemed to eliminate any thoughts of a more permanent relationship.

He rubbed down the animals, gave them some grain and stored the gear before going into the cabin. He was looking forward to a warm night before heading out on the rest of the ride to the forks of the Animas and the problems that awaited. He stoked up a good fire, stripped off his duster and more before stretching out in front of the fireplace. He was enjoying the quiet and warmth when a banging on the door brought him to his feet. With pistol in hand, he stepped to the door and called out, "Who's there?"

"It's me, Marshal, Toots Monroe! Can I come in?"

Cord jerked the door open and motioned the owner of the general store in Wagon Wheel Gap to come inside. As he closed the door, he scowled at Toots, "What's so all-fired important that you'd come up here after dark?"

Toots was one of the earlier settlers of Wagon Wheel Gap and had put in the only general store. The couple had befriended Cord well before he built his cabin that now warmed him on this cold winter night. Cord looked at Toots as he took a chair at the table and dropped his head into his hands, "It's Ma, Mabel, you know, my wife. She's been shot an' might not make it!" he sobbed, shaking his head.

"Well, what are you doin' up here with me? Shouldn't you be down there with her? What happened, anyway?" asked Cord, taking the chair opposite.

"Some men came into town from the gold fields, not prospectors, mind you. Outlaws! One of 'em called himself Bull—big man. He's the one who got upset when Ma told him to pay up! He just up an' shot her! They laughed when she fell, and the three of 'em just walked out, and didn't pay neither!" he sobbed as he remembered. He shook his head and added, "There's a woman, new to the area, one o' the prospectors' wives. She fixed Ma up, bandaged her, and is sittin' with her while I come up here to tell you 'bout it."

"How'd you know I was here? I didn't even stop as I rode through."

"Whitcomb at the livery saw you, told me. He offered to come after you for me, but..." he shrugged, knowing his longtime friend would understand.

"Didn't see 'em, but Whitcomb said they was talkin' 'bout goin' back to Animas Forks."

Cord frowned, "Animas Forks?"

"Yeah, there's been some color showin' up there and they're talkin' 'bout havin' a town. Folks are already callin' it Animas Forks and ain't even a town yet!" grumbled Toots.

"Well, I'd already gotten a complaint about that bunch when I was in Saguache. And...I was on my way to Animas Forks when I stopped off here to have a good night's rest in the warmth of my cabin before takin' out in the morning."

"Same bunch?" asked Toots, frowning.

"Reckon. The name of Bull is the same one that's doin' the leadin' of the bunch. From what I hear, he's been takin' over everything in Animas and thereabouts. Killed a few that resisted so the others either quit resisting or left. You know the story, there's always somebody that thinks it's easier to take it from others than it is to just dig for it."

Cord stood, nodded to Toots, "You need to get back to Mabel. I'll be headin' out early so I'll probably be catching up with 'em even before they get back to Animas Forks, dependin' on the weather, that is."

Toots forced a grin, shook his head, "You got'ny snowshoes?"

"Yeah, an' I'm takin' 'em, but they don't do the horse an' mule any good!" Cord chuckled, his arm around the shoulder of his friend. They shared a time of prayer before Toots left and Cord returned to the fire, shaking his head at the thought of the man losing his life's partner, but she might make it, hopefully, Cord mulled.

THE AIR WAS cold when Cord started down the trail from his cabin, the pack mule reluctantly following and showing his disapproval by dragging his hind feet and grunting and letting loose with an occasional complaining bray. But Kwitcher was the stronger of the two and leaned into the lead rope and dragged the recalcitrant beast behind. Blue was scampering about as if he was enjoying the cooler air, but Cord had his heavier wool lining in his duster and a woolen scarf around his neck and high enough to cover his ears.

A glance to the sky warned Cord that a storm might be on its way and he drew a big sigh at the thought of traveling in the mountains during a blizzard. He had packed extra blankets, wool socks, and another set of red wool long johns as well as the set of snowshoes made for him by John Dyer, the preacher that had married Cord and Tabby. Dyer was often called the Snowshoe Itinerant for his wintertime exploits of traveling his circuit of churches and even carrying the mail through the snowstorms of the Rockies. Cord grinned at the memory of the man and shook his head at his own hesitation for traveling horseback in the early part of winter.

It was second nature for Cord to watch the trail before him for tracks and even though it was cold, the snow still held off and he was hopeful of getting a good sign of the outlaws as they rode north. He had been on the trail just a short time when something unusual caught his eye and he reined up, leaned over for a look at the tracks at the edge of the road and frowned. He shook his head and stepped down for a closer look. Apparently, the travelers before him had stopped here beside the river for a rest stop or just to water the horses and the tracks were easily discernible from the day before. But what stopped Cord was the size of one set of hoof prints, probably the largest he had ever seen. He dropped to one knee beside the tracks, put his spread hand over the top and was startled to see the spread of his hand from thumb to little fingertip, was not quite as big as the hoof print, and the impression was especially deep, indicating the weight of the horse and rider. Where a typical horse hoof print would leave a track about the size of a man's hand with fingers bent, this was considerably larger. Cord shook his head and stood, walked alongside and saw where the rider stepped down and even the rider's boot print was large. And the hobnail boots had a metal rim on the heel that looked like a backward horseshoe, only flat and not quite as big. But the impression was deep and told of the man's considerable size.

Cord looked around, mounted up and started back on the trail, his mind working all the while. As he thought about the horse, he remembered seeing a team of special bred horses that pulled a fancy coach from the east that was carrying some rich industrialist investor who had come west to see the gold prospects. The team was four dapple grey draft horses, they were called, and he also heard someone say they were Percherons, imported from France, and he could not understand why anyone would go to that expense just to have some fancy horses. But they were big and might easily be the same kind as this one ridden by the man who called himself Bull. Cord shook his head, mumbling to himself about how his job just got a lot harder and probably a whole lot more dangerous.

He pulled his collar up, scrunched his head and neck down into his scarf, and hunched his shoulders as the wind began to whistle down the canyon, chasing the howling banshees of winter that rode the whitewater waves of the Rio Grande. It promised to be a perilous journey, and Cord was beginning to wonder what he might be in for, but he had a job to do, and it was time to be about it.

13

CHASE

The Rio Grande River, in cutting its way through the Rocky Mountains, meandered, and bent around the rocky faces, cutting its way along the least resistant path. Springtime with its snowmelt that fed the river, would wear its way down from the higher peaks and would often bring with it much of the mountain, and bringing the worn-away gold that tempted the prospectors. Such was the fluvial terrace that shouldered the west edge of the wide valley, leaving behind temptations for the prospectors to try to dig away at the centuries of snowmelt in hopes of riches. But it was an unusual formation, the lower shoulder that also offered cover from both sight and wind for Cord to travel on this early seasoned, wintry day with the icy wind cutting at any exposed flesh.

Cord hunkered deeper into his coat collar and scarf, letting Kwitcher have his head and pick his own way, the mule occasionally resisting with a pull but usually reluctantly condescending. But both horse and mule stopped suddenly as they neared a small camp of prospectors near the edge of the river. Cord could see a broken rocker box, scattered tools, and two bodies that appeared bloody and broken. The miner's tent had been torn down, personal items scattered, and there were no animals nearby. It appeared the assault had happened the night before, bodies were stiff, eyes wide and staring but dry, and none of the tracks that remained on the windblown terrain, were identifiable. But Cord suspected it was the same bunch of renegades, the murderous bunch of tyrants he was following. He stepped down, gave a closer look to the bodies and searched for anything that would identify the men, but their pockets had been emptied and it appeared anything that was not of value had been tossed onto the campfire that now lay grey and cold. Cord shook his head as he looked about and began doing what he could for the dead, which would be little enough. A small grove of alders and willows and berry bushes offered a bit of cover and he scratched out a shallow grave. He did not take the time to gather the gear and trash but mounted up and started back on the trail.

The tracks stayed on the trail beside the river and Cord was somewhat surprised, believing they would go to Willow, the newer settlement just north of the confluence of the Willow Creek and the Rio Grande River. There had been word of some strikes up that valley, mostly placer claims, but showing good color.

That kind of news usually attracted gold hunters better than honey attracts flies, but the outlaws had elsewhere to go and Cord was on their trail.

Even though the signing of the treaty with the Utes was still a recent thing, the word had quickly spread and the many prospectors and others that had been anxiously awaiting the time when they could freely roam the mountains in their search for gold, had taken to the valleys in that search. Not just the prospectors, but entrepreneurs or investors who had their eyes set on building communities and emptying the pockets of the prospectors either by providing goods or entertainment. Word had already reached Cord about the planting of the settlements of Eureka, Baker's Park, Boullion City, and others and all Cord could do was shake his head and chase the many outlaws and others that wanted to make their money by taking it from the prospectors that did the work.

As the light began to fade and the temperature dropped, Cord had sided the Rio Grande as it swung to the south to make a big bend around the point of hills and push the river against the west edge of the valley. Cord stood in his stirrups to look about, feeling the need for a warm camp and bedroll, and chose to move away from the river and into the edge of the aspen that blanketed the western foothills with the golden aspen. Once into the trees, he spotted a good site that lay in the edge of the spruce and under the slight shoulder of the hills, offering better protection from the wind and good cover for his back with the steep hillside covered with deadfall and branches.

With his belly full of biscuits, bacon, and gravy, Cord rolled out his blankets on the carpet of pine needles and stretched out on the inviting bedroll. With his hands behind his head, the blankets over his body, his pistol under his makeshift pillow, he looked out over the valley, his view framed with the whispering aspen. The wind howled up high, bending the tall spruce and rattling the leaves of the aspen, and Cord shivered as much at the thought of winter as the chill of the high country.

He thought of the men he was pursuing, knowing they were ruthless and daring, but also overconfident. They had left little behind them, no one alive to tell much, but their leavings told Cord most of what he needed to know. They were killers, cruel thieves, and unconcerned about any pursuit or possible consequences of their actions, and that, Cord thought, is what would be their undoing. He rolled over, pulled the covers over his shoulder and with a glance to the horse on one side, the mule on the other and Blue at his feet, he was confident no one could approach without the animals knowing and if they knew, Cord would know.

Two more days on the trail brought him no closer to the outlaws, but he did pass two other camps that had been attacked and destroyed by the renegades. They were leaving a trail of dead bodies without any regard for pursuit or exposure. The trail sided the Rio Grande and continued westward deeper into the San Juans. There were places where the trail had to take to the hills above the deeper canyons and narrow cuts that were too narrow for passage, but seldom was he out of sight of the river. Almost every feeder creek had a camp with prospectors, hopeful of finding their treasure and Cord was surprised to find two camps that had been passed by the outlaws. When he drew near, he paused, raised his free hand high and called out, "I'm friendly! Can I come in?"

He chuckled when he received an answer, "Only if'n you settled things with yore maker! Cuz you try anything, you're gonna be meetin' Him!"

Cord nudged Kwitcher forward, keeping his hands in sight and reined up at the edge of the camp. Two men stood, one on either side of the rocker box, both with double-barreled shotguns. The talker added, "An' if you think you can take us, we got another'n in the trees back yonder with a big Spencer trained on your belly!"

"Whoa now, I'm Marshal Cordell Beckett, and I'm on the trail of some claim jumpers. There's three of 'em, one 'bout as big as a grizzly bear. You seen 'em?"

"You say you the marshal?" he asked.

"Ummhmm," answered Cord, pulling back his duster to show the badge on his vest. "I got word down in Saguache of some bad doin's up to Animas Forks. Been following the bunch after they hit the general store down in Wagon Wheel Gap. You seen 'em?"

"We have, an' after we peppered the trees o'er their heads with buckshot—they decided they wasn't welcome hereabouts so last we seen 'em, they was goin' on up the river!" the miner chuckled.

"How long ago was that?"

"Oh, early this mornin', I was kinda surprised outlaws was up an' about that early, but..." he shrugged.

"Ummhmm, but don't let your guard down. I'm certain they won't be the only ones that wanna get sumpin' for nuthin'," responded Cord.

He nodded to the men and reined Kwitcher around to get back on the trail. It was less than an hour later, and Cord sat at the edge of the Rio Grande River that was nothing more than another typical high-country creek that carried spring water and early snowfall runoff. He watched as five white mountain goats gamboled about in the high reaches of the granite-tipped peaks. A rocky shoulder that would be intimidating to most living things was their playground. It appeared to be a family, one big ram with black horns, a smaller ewe, and two youngsters were playing tag. His attention was caught by the shrill whistle of a whistle pig, or yellow-bellied marmot, and when he looked back, the goats had disappeared over the ridge.

He chuckled as he looked at the white water splashing over the rocks, rushing down the cut between the steep slopes of two granite-tipped peaks that stood tall and proud and well above timberline. He always enjoyed the solitude and quiet of the high country and he was loathe to leave it, but duty called. He looked longingly at the chokecherry and currant bushes that had been bedecked with icicles and the grassy banks that were covered with a thin layer of ice. He thought of Christmas's past when his wife had decorated their home with handmade decorations and he compared these icicles with hers and chuckled at the fond memory. As the trail began to point its way through a bit of a saddle, Cord recognized the area and guessed he was at about 12,000 feet elevation. The sun shone bright and warm, but the air was still frigid. He nudged the big grulla across the little creek, kept to the trail that he knew would take them down into the valley of the Animas River, where Bullion City had been planted.

14

FRIENDS

THE TRACKS FROM THE CLAIM JUMPERS CONTINUED ON THE trail toward the Animas River. Cord stayed on the trail, always watchful and taking his time, as the tracks were no more than a day old and he was cautious about an ambush. But where he rode presently, there was little to hide any attackers, Yet the trail soon dropped into the timber, tall spruce, pine and thickets of aspen. Cord reined up, looked about for any promontory that would afford a better view, but seeing none, nudged Kwitcher to continue down the trail. He had made the first switchback when he spotted more sign, that had come along after the outlaws, but these tracks showed numerous riders of unshod ponies, maybe a hunting party from the Ute. Although the Uncompahgre and Tabeguache were supposed to be traveling south to their newly designated reservation land, it would take them several weeks and they were allowed to hunt as they traveled. Cord knew many of the Ute people and knew their numbers, and it would be a continuous task to keep them all fed.

He looked around for any other sign, hopeful of seeing some of his friends, but there was no one near. He pushed on through the timber, the trail making a zig-zag cut through the timber across the face of the steep mountainside. When he broke into the open it was above a wide deadfall where the standing timber had been flattened, probably the previous winter, by an avalanche, leaving the debris of both aspen and pine that lay humbly flat and pointing to the bottom of the canyon. As the trail circumvented the deadfall, it took to the edge of the timber and as Cord entered the black timber, a soft voice spoke, "You ride the high country alone, do you not know the danger?"

Cord immediately recognized the voice of Lone Eagle, the woman shaman of the Uncompahgre Ute people and a member of the Warriors of the Wolf, the militant arm of the people. Cord reined up, leaned on his pommel and turned to look into the shaded interior of the trees as he watched the woman come from the shadows. She was a beautiful woman, even attired in the everyday clothing of a buckskin tunic over buckskin leggings and with a beaded headband holding her hair back, long braids dangling down her back. The buckskins did little to hide her womanly features and she smiled the coy smile of a beautiful woman who knew her beauty. She held a rifle across the withers of her horse and Cord saw others coming behind her. "Hello Lone Eagle. You and the others hunting in this high country?"

"We are. What brings you here?" she asked, a slow smile painting her face. Both Cord and Lone Eagle remembered the many times they shared with one another from the time she chose Cord as her mate at the spring Bear Dance of the people almost three years past. Chief Ouray had asked Lone Eagle to teach Cord the ways and language of the people so he could be their interpreter when it came time to renegotiate the treaties for the people.

"I'm on the trail of a small band of outlaws. They been hittin' the camps of prospectors, killin' 'em and stealin' ever'thing they got—gold, supplies, horses, and more. They came through here about a day ago," he motioned with a wave to the trail that came from the high country. As they spoke, the others of the hunting party had drawn near, nodding their greetings to Cord, greetings that were returned in kind.

Cord asked, "Are your people camped near here?"

"Our camp is downriver, where the second creek comes from the high country to the north. Your people call it Mineral Creek."

Cord nodded, knowing the location of the valley that split the lower mountains of the San Juans and came from the north. It was a green valley between steep mountains and had been used as a camp by the people for many seasons. "Has Ouray made plans to go south—to the reservation as agreed?"

"We are gathering meat before we go further," explained Lone Eagle as her brother, Broken Arrow, the leader of the Warriors of the Wolf, came alongside. He too had been a friend to Cord for several years and they had hunted together.

Broken Arrow spoke, "Will you come to our camp —have meat with us?"

Cord shook his head and dropped his eyes, wishing he could have time with his friends, but he explained, "No, the men I am after have killed several of the prospectors and they need to be stopped. I believe they will be going upstream to the forks of the Animas, where there are other prospectors and where they are reported to have their cabin."

"Do you need us to come with you? We could help you capture them."

"That is tempting, but no, I'm afraid some of the settlers would get the wrong idea. I think I'll be alright."

Lone Eagle lifted her eyes, "After you get these men, will you stop by our camp if we are still there?"

"Of course, but if you stay too long, you might get a visit from the Buffalo Soldiers. The men at the treaty told of the assignment of the soldiers from the 9th Cavalry at Fort Garland, to come to these mountains and make certain there were no conflicts between the prospectors and your people."

Broken Arrow scowled, "If there are conflicts, it will not be our people that cause them!" His nostrils flared and he tensed his shoulder muscles as he looked at Cord. Even though they were friends, the conflicts between the settlers that broke the treaties, and the Ute who tried to make peace, had been many. But the Ute saw all this part of Colorado Territory as their ancestral lands and had been forced to give up their homes because of those that sought their gold. It was an open sore on the hearts of the people and one that would not soon be healed.

They rode together down Rocky Gulch and on the trail that sided Cunningham Creek, but they parted company at the banks of the Animas River, with the warriors going downstream and Cord turning to the northeast and going upstream. But a small camp of gold diggers at the confluence of the creek and the river stopped Cord. It was another ransacked camp, tools scattered, debris strewn, and one body lying half in and half out of the cold-water creek. It was obviously the recent actions of the same bunch and Cord made short work of burying the body beside a cluster of willows, within sight of Bullion City. Cord finished his work and swung back aboard Kwitcher and turned his back on the afternoon sun and started upriver, bile rising in his throat as his anger boiled within.

Bullion City had a couple of log cabins, one good-sized log building with a porch and a boardwalk and hitchrail in front, and several miners' tents and lean-tos that provided temporary shelter for the gold hunters. Cord reined up in front of the building with a poorly lettered sign that said *Miner supplies, tools, whisky, food. No wimmen.* He slapped the reins and braided lead around the hitchrail, checked the loads in his holstered Colt and the Remington Army in his belt. Stepped up on the boardwalk and pushed through the door into the darkened interior. Heavy cigar smoke filled the air, and a raspy voice came from the back of the one room, "Welcome! What'chu need? Supplies, drink, food...we got'er all!"

Cord paused a moment, letting his eyes adjust to the darker room, and stepped toward the long board that sat across two barrels and held up the elbows of a man with a moustache that drooped over the corners of his mouth and hung well below his chin.

Black eyes peered from under a thick brow and the voice said, "C'mon o'er. I'll git'chu a drink! What'll you have? We got whiskey, whiskey, an' whiskey! Hehehehe..."

"Got'ny coffee?" asked Cord, glancing around the room. Two men sat at the lone table, one man was leaning into the corner, drool coming from his whiskery face and he was obviously asleep or drunk or both.

"It's strong'nuff to float a horseshoe!" declared the barkeep.

Cord nodded, "Sounds like just what I need!" He watched as the man turned to the stove, retrieved the coffee pot and returned to pour a tin cup full of steaming very black coffee. Cord nodded, put a coin on the counter and asked, "You have any strangers come through here last night or this mornin'? Three men, one big as a bear, and a couple others?"

"Why?" asked the barkeep, scowling.

"They been leavin' a trail that I'm followin'," stated Cord, taking a sip of the coffee that almost choked him. He set the cup down, looked at the barkeep who was looking past Cord to the men at the table.

"Hey Hoppy! You see those men he's talkin' 'bout?" asked the barkeep of the men at the table.

"Yeah, stayed shy of 'em too. Why you askin'?"

"I'm tired of diggin' graves," began Cord as he turned sideways to look at the two at the table. "You know the prospector that had a claim down at the confluence of the creek just below here?"

"Yeah, that's Otto, Otto Fisher. Why?"

"That *was* Otto. Just thought somebody might wanna put a marker on his grave."

The two men came to their feet, "Now hold on there! What'chu mean by that?" growled the one called Hoppy. It was quickly evident why he was called such as he hopped to the bar on one good leg and a peg leg. "He's my friend and partner! What happened?"

"I'm guessin' the three men I'm followin' hit his camp, wrecked everything, killed him and took everything of value," drawled Cord, lifting his cup for another sip as he looked at Hoppy over the rim. "Why weren't you in camp with him?" asked Cord.

"I'd been up Porcupine Gulch, done some

pannin', lookin' for better ground. Just stopped in for a drink..." he mumbled, shaking his head and scowling at Cord. "Why you follerin' them three?"

"They've been hitting claims all over. I'm tryin' to catch up with 'em an' put a stop to it."

"Why? You the law or sumpin'?"

"Ummhmmm..." answered Cord. He set the cup down, turned away and left the three men behind, looking at one another, and watching Cord leave.

15

CLOSE

CORD RECALLED THE RECENT HISTORY OF THIS AREA, A LAND rich in stories and even legends of gold finds. Although gold had been originally found a decade past, the presence of the Ute people and the existing treaty at the time, prevented much mining. But the news of the Brunot talks, and even before the treaty, just the report there might be one, had spread rapidly and the influx of gold seekers had picked up like an incoming tide.

It was more than a decade past when gold was first discovered along the Animas River by a group of prospectors led by Charles Baker. But all that had been found then was placer gold, the loose leaf gold found in the streams by panning. It was rich enough, but not enough to risk life for, until more recently when lode gold had been discovered up a gulch that was being called Arrastra gulch. So named because the creek in the bottom carried the placer gold that came from the talus slopes that looked like the remains of an ancient and massive arrastre, or stone grinder mill.

The towering peaks had shed the shale rock in long talus slopes of moss-covered rock of granite and more. It was among these many rocks that a prospector discovered lode gold, or gold in a vein in the rock. It was richer than the placer flakes but also more elusive, yet it beckoned many prospectors that had set up camp in the valley of the Animas and higher in the gulch alongside Arrastra Creek.

Eureka was only about three miles further upstream from Bullion City, and it was showing more signs of growth and a hint of prosperity. Three new log cabins had gone up in the latter part of the summer, a larger log building with a false front was the center of the mountain metropolis with one side being a general store and the other side a tavern and café. Another building was going up that promised to be a livery with a resident blacksmith and ample space for horses and mules inside and outside in the large corral that already stood with a lean-to at the back for shelter for the animals. As Cord approached, he was surprised he had not seen any ransacked camps, but he reckoned that was probably because there were more people around. Few claims stood alone as every foot of the riverbank was sought after and staked out by the many gold hunters, and outlaws prefer to do their deeds without any witnesses around. Such as it has always been since time immemorial, evil does its deeds in the darkness.

The many prospectors were still vigilant, most having rifles or shotguns within easy reach and most often at least one man always standing guard, especially when they saw a stranger approaching. Cord passed them by, going into the town where he could ask around and stand a better chance of actually finding out something without having to use any persuaders in the form of a rifle or a pistol. He spotted the lone business building and nudged Kwitcher to the hitchrail where three other horses were tethered, and Cord stepped down, slapping the reins and lead over the rail and stretching out his lanky body.

"Howdy stranger! New hereabouts?" asked a rumpled-looking man sitting on a chair that leaned back against the wall of the storefront.

"Isn't everyone?" asked Cord, stepping up onto the boardwalk.

"Uh, reckon so. But I ain't seen you aroun' and I know 'bout ever'body!" declared the man who Cord guessed to be over the age of fifty by the grey in his whiskers and what little hair showed from under his floppy hat. "So, let me guess...you ain't a prospector, ain't got the usual far-off look in yore eye an' ain't got no tools on yore pack horse. Ain't a farmer, not enuff stoop to yore shoulders to follow a plow, an' you ain't a trapper, don't stink an' ain't no flies follerin' you. So...just what are you?"

"Mebbe I ain't figgered that out my own self," began Cord, grinning as he leaned back against to center porch post and hooked his thumbs in his gun belt. "Or, maybe I'm just huntin'."

"What'chu huntin'? Ain't showin' no traps an' such, so...you huntin' men?" asked the old-timer, frowning and dropping his chair so the front legs hit the boardwalk and he came forward to drop his elbows on his knees.

"You seen a group of three or more riders, the leader 'bout the size and look of a grizzly bear?"

"You huntin' trouble apurpose?" retorted the old timer, "Or you just like livin' dangerous?"

"So, you have seen 'em. When?"

"Been through here before, but the last time they came through was yestdiddy afternoon. Rode right on by, din't even stop for a drink, which was unusual for them."

"How many?" asked Cord, pulling away from the post and stepping a little closer as he looked at the man.

"Three. Usually more'n that, usually 'bout five of 'em when they's on the prowl. But the other two been hangin' round'chere and when they come through, them other two went with 'em"

"How long they been on the prowl?" asked Cord.

"First heard of 'em 'bout mid-summer. Seems there was a ruckus goin' on upriver. Sumpin' about claim jumpin', killin', you know, such like."

"And they went on through?" queried Cord.

"Ummhmmm...sho'nuff!" answered the old timer.

"How 'bout I buy you a drink?" asked Cord, grinning and motioning to the interior of the tavern and café.

The old man chuckled, slowly rose to his feet and led the way into the store front. As they entered, Cord paused to let his eyes adjust and a voice called out, "So...you found you a sucker did'ju Mose?"

"Mind your manners, young 'un! This hyar's a frien' o' mine!" responded Mose, motioning to Cord as he led the way to a table by the side window.

Mose looked at Cord as they were seated and asked, "Say, young'un, what *is* yore name?"

"I'm Cordell, Cord, Beckett. And you?"

"Mose, or Moses, Appleby. I'm older'n the hills so the name fits, but ain't no apples 'round'chere so I just go by Mose." He paused as he looked around, looked back at Cord, "So, I got the huntin' part right, so why you huntin' them men? They do you wrong or sumpin'?"

"You could say that. I've been followin' a trail they left, gettin' a little tired of diggin' graves everywhere."

"That many?" asked Mose, frowning as he watched the barkeep bring the drinks. He grinned and nodded as the whiskey glass was set before him, but frowned when he saw a tin cup of coffee put before Cord.

Cord nodded to the barkeep, "Thanks, Milt."

"You're welcome, Marshal," responded the grinning barkeep as he turned away with a bit of a glance to Mose.

"Marshal!? You a marshal? Of what?" grumbled Mose, taking a good slug of the whiskey but leaving some for later.

Cord took a sip of the hot black coffee, sat the cup down and grinned at Mose, "Deputy marshal of the third district—that's the southwest corner of Colorado Territory."

"You don't say! Is this a recent happenin'?"

"Nope, been 'bout three, goin' on four years now."

The wide-eyed Mose shook his head and tossed down the last of his whiskey and motioned to Milt for another. He looked over at Cord, "How's come I din't know that?"

"Prob'ly cuz I haven't had to arrest you...yet."

"Don't 'yet' me! You ain't gonna, neither!"

Milt had returned to their table with the coffee pot and refilled Cord's cup, then sat down with the two, grinned as he asked, "So, what'chu lookin' for this time marshal?"

"Not what, but who. The bunch that runs with the fella called Bull. They been wreaking havoc everywhere they go, killin', thievin', and everything else. Worst bunch in a long time."

"They're bad'uns alright. You sure you wanna tangle with 'em? From what I hear, there's at least five of 'em and he seems to be recruitin' more."

"Now that I hadn't heard, recruiting more, huh?" asked Cord, frowning. "You know anything else about 'em?"

"Well, I know they're takin' over everything at the Forks, and anywhere else they go, if they don't take it over, they steal it!" declared Milt, shaking his head and pouring himself a cup of coffee.

"Where do they stay? The Forks don't have a hotel yet, do they?" asked Cord. What the marshal was wanting to learn was if the gang had any patterns to their outlaw ways. Most people unknowingly develop habits or patterns in their ways. Whenever something that is done is successful, they will usually do any repeat action in the same way and thus develop a habit or pattern. Whether it's where they take shelter or perform a task, habits form almost unknowingly and once known, the marshal as a pursuer would gain an advantage in any confrontation.

"Dunno for sure, but I did hear they have a couple cabins up the West Fork a ways."

Cord shook his head, took another drink of coffee and looked at Milt, "Five of 'em, huh?" and looked at Mose as he nodded his head in agreement.

"Well, reckon I better have me a good meal 'fore I go after a bunch like that!" He paused, looked at Mose and asked, "You hungry?"

"I'm always hungry!" responded the old man. With that response and Cord's grin, Milt rose and headed to the kitchen to fetch some plates of stew.

Mose added, "An' if'n yore goin' to the forks of the Animas, I'd like to go along. I got me a claim up there an' muh two young'uns been workin' it. I'd like to see how they's doin'. Y'mind?"

"You have a horse and gear?" asked Cord, surprised at Mose's request.

"Why shore I do! I ain't no pilgrim!" declared the old timer, chuckling.

16

FORKS

"THE TWO MEN THAT ALWAYS RODE IN THE LEAD WERE A mismatched pair. The big man could not be described using the word big, he exceeded that measure by considerable bounds. Although he usually answered to Bull, a better name would be Bear. Even in the summertime, you'd see him wearing or at least carrying a bear skin coat and since he was the size of a grizzly, when he spoke it sounded more like a growl than a conversation. Even his whiskery face resembled that of a bear, and the way he strutted around was more like a bruin than a bull." The barkeep paused in his description as he wiped the plank counter, "He's a monster of a man, standing at least six and a half feet tall and almost as wide at the shoulders. He'd easily weigh in close to three hundred pounds and it takes a big horse to carry his bulk. The big'un he rides, folks say is what some call a Percheron Cross, whatever that is, but it's big! He's a dapple grey stud that'll stand easily o'er sixteen hands and prob'ly weighs in right at a ton. He's got hooves bigger than the spread of a big man's hand, and one thing for certain, wherever he goes, he'd be easy to track!"

The barkeep, Andy, leaned back against the back counter of the saloon, which was the first building to use the new milled lumber from the sawmill down to the mouth of Mineral Creek. It was a typical two-room building with the main room being the saloon with six tables and chairs, a long bar that was nothing more than long planks over some barrels. The adjoining room served as a general store with the back end being the kitchen for the saloon/café. A lean-to storeroom hung off the back. As the barkeep spoke, Cord thought of the man being the talkative sort but also a good observer of people and their manner and ways. The description he gave of the leader of the outlaws was very picturesque, unusual for most. But Cord knew of the outlaw leader and knew as was the way of many men of evil manner, they willingly followed those that were bigger, badder, and more evil than themselves.

The talkative barkeep of the Sundown Saloon in Animas Forks continued, "An' usually, riding beside Bull you'll see his right-hand man, or as some would put it, his number two, a man called Harvey Raney. He's a dapper dan whereas Bull's the opposite. Raney is always well-groomed, dressed, and clean, and he prides himself on his appearance. I think he believes that makes him superior to all others," he chuckled as he thought of the man, and Cord knew the description was of the typical manner of an arrogant and evil man.

"He usually wears a black suit with a vest and frock coat that's split up the back for riding, pin-striped trousers and black boots with silver-mounted big-roweled spurs—yessir, a genuine Jim Dandy! An' he tops it off with his flat-crowned and flat-brimmed hat that shades his face an' makes him look even more dangerous. Then he's got that high-stepping black stallion with two front stockings, long mane and tail and a blaze face, why, he's showy enough to make even that outlaw look presentable!"

"What about the others? Anything special about them?" asked Cord, taking a sip of the steaming coffee before him.

"Wal, those two usually ride side by side in the lead, the third man always rides alone. Ever'thing about him, oh, I dunno, I guess he just likes bein' alone. An' that isolation suits his manner, which was usually disagreeable. He's got a thick mop of red hair that shows from under that high-crowned hat, and a thick beard of red whiskers shows him to be an Irishman an' he sits tall in the saddle, surveys the countryside as if he were the ruler surveying his domain. He's broad-shouldered, thick arms and stumps for legs, Billy O'Neil's most often called Irish. The homespun shirt in a faded brown plaid does little to hide that bulging chest and arms, and the wool britches are stretched taut over his big legs. His big hobnail boots get stuffed into the stirrups of the strawberry roan gelding that's ever' bit as tall as Motley's black and where the black strutted, the sure-footed roan just moves easily along and responds to his rider's slightest whim." The barkeep chuckled, poured Cord a warm-up on his coffee and continued. Cord just grinned, he had been told that Andy was a talkative sort, but now he knew the barkeep was also very observant and Cord relished what he was learning from the man.

"Now, them two men that ride together at the end of the entourage, wal that's where they belong an' where they're placed suits 'em cuz they're the dregs of that crew. Jocko Murphy and Burns Hayes are what most would call the step'n'fetchit crew of the band. Any dirty task is always given to one or the other. Murphy, he's slope-shouldered, tall and lean, with receding hair line and buck teeth that protrude even when his mouth is closed and it affects his speech making his words sound slurred. And where the others appear at least a little clean, the other'n, Burns Hays makes up the difference. There seems to be flies always around him, his drooping whiskers having two trails of tobacco juice down to his chest and continuing over his pot belly. His eyes look in opposite directions and when he had a bit to drink, he would twirl his pistol and scare most everybody around cuz he often drops it and it goes off, scarin' ever'body about, and that causes him to cackle endlessly in a way that'll shake his shoulders and causes a few mistakes with his bladder." He cackled at the memory of the pair but continued. "Now together that band always gives the impression of danger an' trouble, and whenever they ride through town, most people quickly find some way to get out of sight and out-of-the way of any shooting or worse."

"Now, that Bull prides himself on their presence causing fear and making people hide out. I'm guessin' that when they ride into any town, he does like he done here. The first thing he would do is stomp into whatever place, business, tavern, or mining operation, and cause some form of ruckus to get everyone's attention and let them know he's now in charge. But hereabouts, we ain't got much quite yet, and most folks're busy up in the mountains, hurryin' up their doin's 'fore the snow flies. But even so, that ain't slowed down them outlaws any."

"You seen them in the last couple days?"

"Nope, an' that suits me just fine! However, I did hear a couple men sayin' they saw 'em ridin' through last night, just 'fore full dark. Prob'ly goin' to that cabin further up the draw yonder."

Cord knew the beginning settlement of Animas Forks had few people and fewer businesses to make the beginnings of a town, but the road from downriver was often crowded with dreamers and prospectors anticipating their soon to be found riches in gold, and cabins were going up and the hillsides seemed to grow new miners tents and lean-tos like weeds, even though the coming of winter would soon chase most of them to lower climes. The hillsides about had already been picked clean of dead timber, most being the remains of previous winters and avalanches. But the black timber, spruce, pine, fir, was rapidly receding as the newcomers cut the nearest trees to build their cabins. Cord also learned about two men named Henry Tower and Wesley Stevens who had chosen to mine the miners instead of the mines and decided to build a sawmill down at Mineral Creek to mill the lumber needed for the many buildings that would be in demand. But with the coming of winter, building was slowing, prospecting was beginning to wane, and the cold air whistled through the valley to warn of the coming of old man winter.

Cord finished his coffee, watched as Andy moved down the plank bar to greet and tend to two men that had stood at the end of the bar. Andy poured them a drink, glanced to Cord and with a questioning look that asked if he wanted more coffee, Cord declined but leaned on the bar as he looked around. He heard the men talking about claims, prospecting, milling and more. These were not the typical 'dig in the dirt' prospectors, but these men were miners that had set about finding the veins and going after the lode gold. These two, Albert Burrows and Charles McIntyre, had become well known in the area and had staked several claims in the upper reaches of the headwaters of the Animas River. They had been talking about their claims and Cord moved closer, interrupted the men and asked, "You men been roaming the mountains around here for a while, have you?"

The two frowned, looked at the man who was a stranger to them, and McIntyre asked, "Why you askin'? Don'chu know it's none o' yore business?" he growled.

"I'm not bein' nosy, just concerned." He opened his duster to show his vest and the badge, "I'm investigating some outlaw doin's hereabouts. Seems there's a bunch of men that think they can take over any and all claims and run off the owners. They've killed a few in the doin' of it, and I just wanted to know if you've run into 'em?"

"You talkin' 'bout that bunch that's led by the big'un they call Bull?" asked Burrows.

"That's the bunch," nodded Cord. "You seen 'em?"

"Not recently. We've been in the high country, haven't run into 'em. But we've heard about 'em. One fella said they had a cabin up the West Fork a ways. He said he had a claim up thataway, but they run him off. Now, Marshal, that was a claim duly filed and recorded, and no matter what they do, unless the claimant is dead or gone..." he shrugged.

Cord slowly shook his head and lowered his eyes, then looked at the two with a frown, "That's prob'ly why they're killin' the claim holders. It's been reported they plan to take ‘em over, but I doubt they’ll work any of them. They’re not the type. But they’ll probably try to sell ‘em to newcomers anxious to see some color.”

“What’chu gonna do?” asked McIntyre.

“Find ‘em, put a stop to it—somehow. Don’t rightly know how that’s gonna happen, but...” he shrugged, grinned, and turned away with a nod to the barkeep before he walked out the door.

17

SURVEY

IT HAD BEEN SOME TIME SINCE CORD HAD BEEN IN THIS area and he decided he would make a circuit ride hereabouts, just to know the lay of the land and the location of most of the claims and working mines. When he walked out from the Sundown Saloon, he stood on the stoop and looked about, and chose to take to the high country at the headwaters of the Animas River, circle about and making it back to the West Fork and maybe finding the cabin of the outlaws and the cabin of Mose and his claim. He chuckled as he thought of Mose, they had parted company as they neared the basin with the forks of the Animas, with him taking a trail to the west and into the valley of the West Fork, while Cord continued on into the basin and the site of the making of what would become the town of Animas Forks.

Now he swung aboard Kwitcher, looked up at the

sun to see it was late morning and still had a bit to go before the high noon sun. He nudged Kwitcher away from the rail, motioned Blue to take the lead and they headed out of town passing the livery, the beginnings of another building that was planned as a café, and the skeleton of another that was said to be a hotel or boarding house. He nudged Kwitcher toward the break between the mountains on the east and chose to take the trail that sided the North Fork, high up on the shoulder on the East Side.

The sun was warm, the air cool, and the sky a brilliant blue. It was a typical fall day in the Rockies with this trail hanging on the side of the mountain at timberline. Yellow flowers known as Old-man-on-the-Mountain decorated the hillsides together with some Stonecrop and Western Wallflower. The splotches of yellow decorated the clumps of green grasses and moss rock that fell from the talus slope. The opposite hillside had the shade-loving fir that tried their best to climb higher, but the cold weather, hard rock, and unforgiving climate prevented their climb.

Below the trail, the mountain creek splashed white water between icy banks, determined to make it to the lower climes. As Cord looked about, the hillsides were pock marked with prospect holes of hopeful miners, but every so often, stakes showed the presence of a claim and whenever Cord went to check out the claims, he noted that almost all the claims in these upper reaches of the North Fork were marked by Albert Burrows and Charles McIntyre and others by Reuben McNutt and George Howard. These were names that were known in the valley and were men who had been successful in their prospecting. Many of the claims were also named showing such titles as Big Giant, Bill Young, Bonanza, Boston, Burrows, and Red Cloud.

He came to the crest and the Continental Divide, recognizable when the headwaters of the other creeks headed off down to the Western slope and turned to the west to take the game trail beside Burrows Creek and here, even on the back side of Houghton Mountain, prospect holes marked the center of claims or the dashed hopes of prospectors. He kept to the trail for a couple miles, nudged Kwitcher to the south toward the low saddle between the two mountains, and followed the faint game trail, probably made by migrating elk, over the saddle and down the long slope to the valley of the West Fork. When he neared the creek, it had very little water, some ice, and the grassy bottom that showed signs of prospectors trying their luck in the little stream.

Further up the long draw, Cord saw the peak of the roof of a log cabin that was as much dug-out as it was cabin, but the corral beside it held several horses and he guessed this was the retreat of the outlaws. He was not ready for a confrontation, not when he was alone and there were five of them, so he nudged Kwitcher downstream and around the bend of the big rocky shoulder to drop into California Gulch, where he believed he would find Mose and his two sons busy at his claim.

Last season's snow still showed in the folds of the mountainside, already dusted by the early snows of the fall. The faces of the slopes were heavy with slide rock and moss rock of granite, the bottom of the valley holding the little stream bounded by currant and kinnikinnick bushes. The blue sky held a handful of white clouds and the cold air made Cord hunker into his collar. But it was a serene landscape, the only scars made by the prospect holes that showed yellow and rust on the grey-faced hillsides. Near the entry to the California Gulch, a cabin and a larger building told of the makings of a lode ore operation, the dump stretching out to the end of the building that obscured the opening to the mine.

Further up the valley, Cord saw the peak of the roof of a cabin, and by the description given by Mose, that would be the cabin of his sons. Cord grinned and pointed Kwitcher that direction, watching as Blue investigated the trail before them. He glanced to the sky, and both the high-up sun and the growling in his stomach told him it was already past noon time and whatever waited in the cabin was less important than getting something to eat. Cord grinned, took a deep breath and nudged Kwitcher to a quick step trot.

The road held to the shoulder of the west slope, the heavy and oftentimes massive boulders protruding or even hanging on the steep face of the mountain. Whenever there was a cut in the horizon, a talus slope paved the way for spring runoff or offered a path for avalanche in the deep of winter when the snow would reach well over twenty feet deep. This was above timberline and the altitude was cold with thin air at almost 12,000 feet.

Kwitcher took tenuous steps as they crossed the precipitous talus slope, but once across, they were welcomed by the sight of the log cabin that fit the description given by Mose, but Cord noticed there were no horses about, although there was a small corral with a lean-to shed behind the cabin.

As he neared, a frowning Cord saw the sign of several horses, most tracks going to and from the corral, but once leaving the corral, the tracks took a well-traveled trail further into the gulch. Cord believed that to be where the claim was and Mose had said it was a lode claim, which meant they were digging deep into the face of the mountainside, pursuing what they thought was a rich gold-bearing vein. But there was nothing further up the gulch that held any interest to Cord, but the possibility of a coffee pot hanging over the fire in the fireplace inside was tempting.

After picketing the horse and mule, stripping off the gear, and rubbing them both down, Cord carried his saddlebags inside and grinned when he saw the coffee pot hanging over the cold ashes of the fire. Within a short while he had the fire going, coffee pot refilled with both water and coffee, and a couple strips of venison sizzling over the fire. He stepped to the door, stood in the sunshine and looked about. The mountainsides were pockmarked with prospect holes, and even from this distance, Cord could see where stakes had been placed to mark the boundaries of claims. He walked out into the trampled grass and casually looked at the tracks and paused, bent down for a closer look, and saw the unmistakable tracks of the big horse ridden by Bull. As he stood, he looked at the sign about the cabin, but there was nothing that told of a conflict or fight of any kind, but the big tracks took to the trail. Cord followed the tracks to the trail and saw where the big horse and others had gone south, deeper into the valley, but there were more recent tracks leaving the valley.

Cord sauntered back to the cabin, frowning and thinking, wondering just what had happened further up the valley. If the band of outlaws pursued Mose and his boys, had there been a confrontation? And if so, what had happened? But the tracks indicated the group had traveled over the trail after Mose and company, and returned before Mose returned, since Mose and family were still absent from the cabin. He had heard no gunfire, nor saw any sign of any fight, but that did not mean nothing happened.

Cord walked back into the cabin, still thinking and considering and as he did, he was also trying to remember anything Mose had said about the claim, but he also recalled that Mose had seemed to be purposely evasive as to the location of the claim. And this was big country to try to find one claim, especially if the mine was very deep and the workers not easily found.

He made short work of his meal and finished off the coffee before cleaning up and packing up. He had decided he had to at least take a look in the upper end of the basin, just to make sure there was nothing amiss. He owed that much to Mose, even though their friendship could be counted in days.

It was just a little more than a mile to the upper end of the valley of the West Fork, a bowl of a basin was wrapped in steep walls with rimrock on the east side, and taller peaks with talus slopes on the west side. In the face of the cliffs, a shaft had been dug, leaving a dump pile that cascaded down the slope to the bank of the little creek below. The tracks of the big horse and others were abundant near the opening of the shaft, but there was no evidence that anyone had dismounted until after they moved away from the shaft, further up the beginning of a switchback trail that mounted the end of the basin. The sign showed where two or three riders had continued up the trail, but the big horse and another had stopped, their riders dismounted and appeared to wait a while for the return of the others.

The switchback led higher and into a smaller basin, with the trail turning back to the east and moving toward Picayune Gulch or split to go to

Eureka Gulch. Cord did not follow, noticing the return of the two riders that joined the big horse and the others and returned down the valley of the West Fork of the Animas. Still no sign of where the claim of Mose and his family lay, and no sign of the outlaws finding it either. Cord paused, stepped down and with field glasses in hand, seated himself on the slope and scanned the basin and the steep hillsides and more, looking for any giveaway for the claim of Mose, but nothing revealed itself.

Cord climbed back aboard, and reluctantly started back down the trail, heading for Animas Forks and hopefully learn a little more about the doings of the outlaws. He was hopeful that the increasing number of prospectors or at least the coming of winter might be a discouragement to their shenanigans, as most outlaws are not too anxious to get involved in hard work and definitely not in cold weather. But it was his task to track them down and put a stop to their ways, one way or another.

18

CONFRONTATION

As he neared town, he was surprised to hear the sounds of construction and saw several men appearing like bees in a hive buzzing about the larger of the building projects that was supposed to become a hotel. He glanced to the sky, a clear blue canopy with the warm and bright sun standing high above without the company of any clouds. It was one of those unseasonably warm and sunny days not often found in the high country at this time of year. But Cord knew the weather could change quickly and the next day could see nothing but a blanket of white laying peaceful and serene and sparkling with that same sunshine. But his concern was not about the weather. He had that prickly sensation crawling up his back that warned of some kind of trouble.

The workers paid no attention to the man on the grulla and leading a pack mule, he was little different from the many others that had followed the clarion call of gold and was given no heed. He glanced around, saw the pockmarked hillsides with the many prospect holes and ore dumps that told of unfulfilled hopes. But he knew that come spring, there would be more and the hills would be alive with many scampering prospectors as well as the proven claims developing into full operating mines. There were already a couple mines that had begun producing and had buildings to house the bigger equipment needed for the lode mining operations and he had heard about the coming of the Dakota and San Juan Mining company who were planning to put in a large mill. He was hopeful the presence and addition of the bigger mines and companies would discourage the outlaw bands that preyed on the smaller miners and prospectors, but for now, it was a problem to be resolved. He turned to the livery and hailed the smithy at the doorway. When the smithy stepped into the sunlight and wiped his hands on his leather apron and growled, “What’chu need?”

“How ‘bout puttin’ my animals up a day or two, an’ if you have room in your loft for me’n my bedroll?” asked Cord.

“Shore, but you ain’t plannin’ on stayin’ thru the winter are ye?” asked the smithy.

Cord chuckled, slowly shaking his head, “No, sir! I got me a cabin down by Wagon Wheel Gap and that’s about as high as I care to be, come snowfall!”

"Got room fer a boarder?" asked the grinning whisker-faced smithy.

"No, made it little apurpose!" Cord chuckled, swinging down from his saddle. The smithy motioned to several open stalls and Cord led Kwitcher and the mule into the dimly lit interior. He called over his shoulder, "Been any trouble in town lately?"

"What kinda trouble?" growled the smithy, frowning at Cord's back.

As Cord put the animals in the stall and began stripping the gear, "Oh, you know, fights, killin', claim jumpin', such like."

"What's it to you?"

Cord chuckled, "I'm the territorial marshal."

"Oh, din't know that. Why ain't we seen you afore?"

"Oh, I've been through, just didn't have any reason for spending any time here. But..." he shrugged.

"So you know 'bout some o' the trouble?"

"Ummhmm," replied Cord, then nodded across the way to the opposite stalls where several horses stood with heads in the haymows, "like from the riders of those horses there."

"They're trouble sure'nuff! Specially the one that calls himself Bull. He's the boss o' the bunch an' they do whatever he tells 'em."

"They been 'round long?"

"Just the last couple months. Came in long with a

bunch o' prospectors. He din't have all them fellas with him then, but it din't take him long to find 'em. Like muh momma used to say 'bout *Birds of a feather* but she usually added *they stink together* instead of sticking together. And in this case, she was right. Ain't been nuthin' but trouble since they showed up!"

"Where might they be now?" asked Cord.

"Prob'ly o'er to the Sundown. That's where most folks go, an' there's a fella has a cabin up the hill behind it that he lets some roll out their bedrolls for a price." He paused, waited for Cord to finish tossing some hay to his horse and mule, and when Cord came into the light from the big open door, the smithy added, "I saw you when you left earlier, and it was a while after that they come into town. Been o'er to the Sundown since, oh, maybe an hour or more 'fore you came."

Cord nodded, glancing from the smithy to the Sundown Saloon and back. He had stashed his gear in the corner of the stalls, returned and retrieved his Greener shotgun and a pocketful of shells, then returned to the smithy's side. "Anything in particular I should know before I do this?"

"Ummhmm, you oughta know Jesus on a real personal level. Do you?" growled the smithy, frowning at the marshal who he was questioning regarding good sense.

Cord chuckled and grinned, "Yessir, I do. I have accepted Christ as my Savior and I know I'm goin' to

Heaven...I just don't know how soon!" He stepped off, laying the Greener over one shoulder and slipping the thong off the hammer of his Colt that sat holstered on his left hip, butt forward, and touching the butt of the Remington Army in his belt to loosen it to move freely. He took a deep breath that lifted his shoulders and he stepped up on the boardwalk under the overhang of the building and stood before the swinging doors to look into the dim interior. He stepped inside, moved to the side to let his eyes become accustomed to the faint light, and with a nod to Andy who stood behind the plank bar, stepped to the bar and lay the shotgun on the plank.

"Afternoon, Cord! Din't 'spect you back so soon. You find your friends?" he asked, and Cord noticed he did not refer to him as Marshal and he glanced a little nervously to the side by way of warning Cord of the others in the room.

Cord let a slow grin paint his face and gave a bit of a nod to tell Andy he was aware of the others and he answered the barkeep with, "No, no, I didn't, Andy. I reckon they're out prospectin' somewhere, but I saw a lot of country hereabouts. Say, how 'bout some hot coffee to warm up muh innards?"

"Sure Cord, we got some on the stove—let me fetch it for you," answered Andy as he turned to go to the stove.

Cord slowly turned sideways to lean one elbow on the bar, but kept access to his pistol as he looked about. His duster covered the pistol in his belt and the holstered pistol was also out of sight. He looked about the interior, saw three of the four tables with men gathered around, most just hunkered over, talking. But one table had a card game going and the men were a little more attentive to one another. The fourth table was the one with the outlaws, the big man, Bull, sitting in the corner with his back to the wall and he leaned forward, elbows on the table, looking about as if this was his domain and he was the ruler of everything and everyone.

Cord had turned back to the plank bar when Andy returned with his coffee, and Cord accepted the offered cup, reaching for and anticipating the tasty brew.

But the growling shout from behind him resounded through the room and everyone paused and looked at the big man as he came to his feet, "Hey you! At the bar! C'mere now!"

Cord glanced quickly to Andy, whose eyes flared and showed a mixture of fear and anger. The barkeep started to respond, but Cord lifted his hand to stop him. Cord intentionally ignored the shout and lifted the cup to his mouth but watched the crowd behind him in the mirror behind the bar. He saw the big man, Bull, standing at the table in the corner, his massive paw lifted as he did his best imitation of a bear and growled again, "I'm talkin' to you at the bar! C'mere!"

Cord sipped his coffee, sat the cup down and rested his elbows on the bar as he breathed deeply and lifted his shoulders in the doing. He grinned as he glanced at Andy, watching the reaction of the barkeep to let him know what was happening out of sight of the mirror. When Andy looked again at Cord, and moved his eyes quickly to the big man in the corner, Cord knew the man was on the move. Cord slowly turned, leaned back against the bar but let his duster drape open allowing him access to both pistols, and he grinned at the people, looking around and frowning, slowly letting his eyes settle on the big man, Bull. But Cord did not respond, just frowned.

"I tol' you to c'mere!" growled the big man.

Cord just gave a slight nod, and turned his back on the man without answering. In the mirror he saw the other four men at the table slide their chairs back away from the table, and the two men nearest Bull slowly stood, pushing their chairs back, while the other two stood and stepped away. Cord slowly moved the butt of the shotgun near Andy and with his head lowered as if he was reaching for his coffee, he spoke quietly to Andy, "Keep the others off me."

"You comin'?" Bull growled again.

Cord frowned, slowly turned back to face the man and asked in a quiet voice, "You talkin' to me?" and touched his chest as he frowned, letting his frock coat drape open allowing access to his pistols. "Surely not—because when you talk to me you need to show some manners. You know, like sayin' please and thank you, *sir*!"

The retort instantly angered the big man and he

growled as he hunkered his head down, snatched the edge of the table and tossed it aside and angrily pulled off his bearskin coat, dropping it to the floor and stomped toward Cord, who stood frowning and watching. As the big man neared, Cord grinned and asked, “You come to say please, did’ju?”

19

ENCOUNTER

CORD'S REPEATED BARBS AND TAUNTS HAD ACCOMPLISHED just what he wanted—to get the man so riled and angered he would lose control. The big man did like he probably had done many times before to intimidate any opponent, he stomped, growled, did his best imitation of a bear with his flexed massive arms and started to charge. Cord knew the big man would attempt to pin him against the bar, and use his strength and size to destroy Cord with a bear hug or some similar move, but Cord was prepared. With what he had learned and repeatedly applied in the way of Muay Thai, the Capoeira, and even the skills of the hand fighting of the Ute people, Cord *was* prepared.

When the man charged, Cord came erect, dropped into a slight crouch and as the big man came within reach, Cord spun around, using his lower leg and heel to sweep the man's feet from under him. The monster dropped on his back with a thud that shook the building and every glass and bottle on the back bar. But the big man, surprised to find himself on his back, quickly rolled to the side and came to his feet. His speed surprising Cord, but Cord had stepped back and dropped into a bit of a crouch again, watching the man as he rose to his full height. Cord estimated his height to be at least six and a half feet tall, and his weight to easily exceed three hundred pounds, making Cord realize the resemblance of Bull to an actual bear.

But Cord had shrugged off his duster and tossed his hat to the bar, stood with hands lifted at his side and began to sidestep away from the bar and into the open space on the floor. The other men had already moved tables and chairs aside and stood around, anxious to see the fight. Again Bull charged Cord, grunting and grumbling as he moved, eyes flaring and mouth wide, and seeming to block any escape with his outstretched arms, growled, "I'm gonna tear you apart! Then I'm gonna roast yore hide on the fire!"

Cord let a grin split his face and asked, "You gonna do that by talkin'?"

The taunt did its work and the man charged, but his arms caught nothing but air and as he passed, Cord chopped down on the back of the man's neck with both hands clasped and as he did, he brought up a knee to the midriff of the beast. Air expelled from his mouth as he flailed for air and something to grab, but there was nothing and he sprawled on his belly on the rough plank floor with a thud that rocked the building. He came to his hands and knees, shaking his head, and turned to look at Cord who now stood leaning against the bar, sipping his coffee.

Bull came to his feet, his lips snarling, his eyes squinting, and he growled at his men, "Kill him!" motioning to Cord. But the clicks of two hammers cocking on the big Greener shotgun stayed the movement of the four men as they looked at a grinning Andy with the big shotgun in hand as he leaned on the plank bar, shaking his head and saying, "No, not today, boys!"

The four men knew the spray of a double-barreled ten-gauge shotgun at that range would leave no one alive and everyone nothing more than a bloody pulp. They slowly lifted their hands high and looked back to Bull.

Cord chuckled, "Thanks, Andy!" then turned to Bull, "You were saying?"

Bull roared and charged again, arms stretched wide and his eyes glared, thinking he had Cord pinned against the bar and the corner of the wall, but Cord stepped toward him, meeting his charge and as the big man grabbed, Cord came high off his feet, grabbed the back of Bull's long hair and jerked his face down to meet Cord's knee as he brought it up to smash the face of bull. Then he kicked the big man in the middle, pushing him down onto his back on the floor with another thundering thud. Cord stepped aside, now breathing heavy, and wiped his face. Bull's head had caught Cord's face and bloodied his nose, but nothing bad.

But Bull thought he had hurt Cord and when he came to his feet, the sight of Cord's blood gave new life to his fight, and he laughed a mocking laugh as he roared, "Now you're mine! I'm gonna stomp you into dead meat!" and dropped into a crouch and charged. Cord stepped back and his foot struck a spittoon that tipped and spun, spilling its ilk on the floor and Cord slipped. The big man grabbed at Cord's clothes, getting a handful as Cord fought for footing, but the big man's charge carried them both to the floor.

The beast was on top of Cord and his weight seemed to crush his chest. The massive arms of Bull pinned Cord's to the side and when Bull inched forward, his huge legs were pinning Cord even tighter to the floor. The foul stench of Bull's breath and the slobbers from his whiskers were choking Cord, and the big man used his forehead to smash down toward Cord's face, but he turned enough to take the blow on his cheekbone, yet it felt like the bone broke with the impact. Bull growled, chuckled with a huff and a snarl, pinned both Cord's arms to the floor as he lifted his head and chest so he could glare at the marshal.

He started to laugh but Cord saw something moving behind the big man and a wide-armed chair was lifted high above and came crashing down on the back of the beast, smashing the back of the Bull's head and neck, driving it to the floor beside Cord's head. Some of the splinters of the chair hit Cord's face but were harmless. Cord dared to try to breathe and Bull's weight was restrictive, but Bull was not moving. Cord struggled, pushing against the dead weight, and finally someone else was helping and he crawled from under the monster.

When Cord came to his feet, he looked about for whoever had used the chair and was surprised to see no one near except a woman. She stood, hands on hips, a snarling glare on her face as she looked at the inert form of Bull and noticed the back of his head had been smashed in, apparently by the hardwood seat of the chair and a pool of blood had formed that now dripped down the side of his neck, but he was not moving. Cord looked from the form of Bull to the chair and to the woman. She was no more than five feet tall, probably weighed less than a hundred pounds and wasn't much bigger than the chair. He marveled that such a little wisp of a woman could even heft the chair, much less use it as a club and swing it overhead. The woman appeared to be more of a young girl than a woman but she had long reddish-blonde hair that hung loosely over her shoulders and a shapely figure that showed even though she wore men's trousers and shirt with a loose hanging buckskin jacket.

Cord, frowning, looked at the young woman who he guessed to be a somewhere around twenty years old, and asked, "Did you smash that chair on his head?"

She turned to look at Cord, nodded, "Ummhmm...he'n his men kilt my father and my brother. I came huntin' him to kill him!" She accented the statement with a stern expression, a nod of her head and a stab of her chin.

Cord looked wide-eyed at her, then turned to look at the still form of Bull, and back to the woman, "Darned if you didn't! Who was yore Pa?"

"Mose, Moses Appleby. We have a claim up the West Fork. They came up there yestiddy, jumped Pa an' my brother went to help him. Made me stay in the mine. When I came out after, they were both dead. Shot, robbed, and left. I come after 'em. Nothing else I could do."

"What's your name?" asked Cord.

"Ema, Emaline Appleby. Why?"

"I knew your pa. I thought he had two sons, never said he had a daughter. We came up here together. I went to your cabin earlier and looked for you, but...well, I rode around some, didn't find your claim, came on back to town."

"You the marshal he talked about?"

"I am." He extended his hand, "I'm Marshal Cordell Beckett, pleased to meet'chu."

Emaline dropped her eyes, smiled widely and looked back up, twisting a little in her movements and accepted Cord's hand and shook it, and held on to it as she asked, "What are you gonna do with them?" nodding toward the others that still stood, watching, keeping their eyes on the double-barreled shotgun.

Cord grinned, stepped to the bar and took the shotgun. He looked at the four, "You fellas just slowly unbuckle your gun belts and get rid of any hideouts, and then we'll talk about your future."

They did as they were told, cautiously moved their hands to the buckles of the gun belts, carefully watching Cord, and the two on the right side, who Cord pegged as Burns Hayes and Jocko Murphy, eagerly complied and unbuckled and dropped their hardware. But the other two sidestepped apart and the one on the far left was the redhead known as Irish and Cord had been told he was probably the most dangerous. Cord grinned and followed his movement with the muzzle of the shotgun and explained, "Now, you can try, but there has never been a man quicker than my trigger finger and the blast from just one barrel will carry you out that window and they won't find all your parts till some time next spring, so, go ahead if you think you can do it."

And he thought he could, but Cord was watching his eyes and knew the eyes, the gateway to the soul, would always be the giveaway. With an involuntary slight squint, Irish tried to bring his pistol to bear, but Cord dropped the hammer on the shotgun and the blast filled the room. Double aught buckshot made a bloody pulp of the middle of the Irishman and drove him back into the crowded tables and chairs, splintering and crashing into a heap.

Cord had expected the other man, Raney, to make his move first, but the man was smart enough to let the Irishman take the first load, believing the move would give him time. But he was mistaken for that was exactly what Cord had expected and he had already cocked the hammer on the second barrel and a quick twist of his hip brought the muzzle to the fancy frock coat and buck shot aerated the well-groomed outlaw, smashing him against the end of the bar, but he still tried to raise his pistol and Cord's Colt chased the buckshot with a pair of .44 caliber slugs that tattooed the remaining white shirt collar at the man's throat.

Gunsmoke filled the room and lay like a wispy blanket over the quiet where no one moved. Cord slowly lowered the muzzle of his pistol, holstered the weapon and held the shotgun in the crook of his arm as he broke open the action and reloaded both barrels. The remaining two outlaws, Murphy and Hayes, stood watching wide-eyed, unmoving. When Cord snapped the shotgun closed, he looked around the room as the others began moving chairs and tables back in place and he spoke loud enough for all to hear.

"Men—this bunch has been murdering miners and jumping claims all around this area. You saw what those three tried," nodding to the bodies on the floor, "and these two were a part of the bunch. They killed at least eight, no ten, counting this lady's dad and brother, that I know of and they need some judgement brought. Now, I can do one of two things. I can either take 'em down river to Judge James Belford, the circuit judge, and have a trial. Or you men can get your miner's court together and do what's right. What say?" he asked, looking around the room.

The men looked at one another, mumbled to each other and looked back at Cord and one man stood, looked at Andy, "Andy, can we use your saloon for a courtroom?"

"Sure you can! I'll even provide whatever might be needed!"

The man looked at the others, back to Cord, "We'll put the word out and if you can lock 'em up some'eres, we'll hold court on 'em tomorrow when we have more men here. That alright?"

"That'll be fine." He looked at Andy, "Where can I lock 'em up?"

Andy grinned, "Storeroom's back there—go 'head on."

Cord looked at Ema and asked, "Would you wait till I get rid of some baggage?"

She smiled and nodded, went to a table and pulled out a chair and watched as Cord took the two men to the back room.

20

TRAVELING

Chad Currington was the chairman of the Miner's Court, and he demanded attention when he slammed down the hand sledge on the plank to get everyone's attention. He stood behind the plank bar of the Sundown Saloon and looked at the men. At the sudden thud of the sledge, a few jumped, a couple spilled some of their beer, but everyone looked to the chairman and waited for his direction. "Men, this court is gonna be a mite different than what we're used to—ain't got nuthin' to do with filin' a claim, but it's got a lot to do with our claims and work." He paused, looked around the main room of the Sundown Saloon at the men that were seated at the tables and standing around the walls.

"These two that sittin' down here," he said as he nodded to the two men that were tied to the chairs with ropes behind their backs and facing the chairman, "are accused of murder of at least ten men, all miners workin' their claims. And they're also accused of stealin' claims and pokes and other things belongin' to the murdered men.

"Now, we ain't gonna take the time to try to hear 'bout every one of the victims, cuz we got us a prime witness here to account for their most recent murderin' spree and thievery." He paused, looked around the room and when he spotted Cord, he nodded and continued. "We have Territorial Marshal Cordell Beckett with us an' he's been follerin' these men, buryin' the murdered miners, and chasin' after these and the others that were with 'em. Now, most of you have heard 'bout the shootin' yestiddy. The marshal there had a run-in with the leader and a couple others of this gang and he already passed sentence on them. Now we got these two," he paused to look at a piece of paper before him and read the names, "Burns Hayes and Jocko Murphy, they're the last two of the gang, and they're on trial today."

The chairman looked at Cord and said, "Now, we'll hear from the marshal first." He nodded for Cord to begin his report.

Cord stood, cleared his throat, and began relating what he knew about the gang, the different claims they had attacked and the miners killed. As he related the different attacks, several of the men mumbled, some knowing the men or shared their familiarity of the claims and claimholders, even sharing personal information about the dead. Cord made his report as brief as possible and wrapped it up with, "But we have Emaline Appleby here as a witness as to their attack on the claim of her family." He nodded to Ema, motioning for her to stand and look at the chairman.

The chairman directed, "Ma'am, you just tell us what you can, but just the facts of what happened. Will that be alright?"

Ema forced a bit of a smile, nodded and stilled herself before beginning. She looked around the room, and began, "Men, some of you know our claim, the claim of my father Mose, my brother Everett, and me. It's on the upper end of the West Fork on the north side. It's a lode claim and it has been showing good color. Me'n my brother have been workin' it every day and we've brought in some good ore. Pa came to see us an' see how we've been doin' and those men," she pointed at the two men on trial, "and the other three with 'em, followed Pa. When he came into the mine, he'd just been there a short time when they hollered out for Pa and he went out. He'd no sooner come into the daylight and we heard gunshots. My brother ran out, they shot him too. But Pa an' muh brother told me to stay in the mine, no matter what, and that's what I done, till I heard the sounds of them outlaws leavin'. When I went out, I found muh pa and brother both dead, shot many times, and their pokes was gone too.

"After I buried 'em, I followed the tracks of the bunch into town here. It was easy to track that big horse of Bull, we'd seen them before. When I got here, there was a fight goin' on and I came in, saw Bull tryin' to kill the marshal by squashin' him. I was still mad, an' nobody was doin' nuthin', so I grabbed up one o' these big chairs an' broke it o'er his head! Killed him too!" She pursed her lips showing her determination and anger as she looked around the room.

"After he got up, the marshal that is, he was forced to kill two o' th' others but kept these two for you men to hang!" At her statement of hanging, the room broke into boisterous shouts and expressions of anger at the outlaws, but most agreed that they were guilty and should be hanged.

The chairman, in an attempt to bring order to the room, repeatedly banged the sledge on the plank, splintering the long board end-to-end, and the boisterous crowd laughed at the predicament of the chairman, but he slammed the sledge down on the remnant of the plank and shouted, "Order! Order! Quiet down! We gotta pass sentence!"

The turmoil settled down somewhat until one of the miners shouted, "They's guilty! Hang 'em!" and the call was repeated by most of the others until the chairman again tried to bring order. His banging preceded his shout, "Alright! Alright! They're guilty! Hang 'em!"

One of the men shouted, "Where? Where we gonna hang 'em?"

The crowd of men looked at one another, several making suggestions, none acceptable, until one man said, "How 'bout the derrick of the Blue Bonnet?" He spoke of the overhead derrick frame that lowered the ore bucket into the mine shaft of the Blue Bonnet mine, one of the earliest diggings in the area.

The men looked at each other, each thinking about the derrick, and almost as one, the shout went up, "Yeah! That'll do it! Let's go!"

Cord looked to the chairman who nodded his agreement and pronounced, "These two men, Burns Hayes and Jocko Murphy, are now pronounced guilty of the murder of Moses Appleby and his son, Everett Appleby, and are sentenced by this Miner's Court to be hanged by the neck until dead! All in agreement, say guilty!"

The crowd roared in unison, "Guilty!" Several of the leaders took the initiative and went to get the men from the chairs. Cord glanced to the chairman who nodded his approval and Cord stepped back to let the prisoners be taken for their sentence.

CORD'S RESPONSIBILITY ended with the sentence of the Miner's Court and he was not interested in watching the carrying out of the hanging. He stayed behind, concerned about Ema and asked her to join him and stay for something to eat and talk. They were seated at the table by the window and had just spoken with Andy about the meal when a man pushed through the door, looked around the room and when he saw

Ema at the table, he approached, removing his hat as he neared.

"Excuse me, ma'am, could we talk a moment?" he asked, nodding to the extra chair at the table.

She glanced at Cord and back to the man and said, "Uh, I s'pose. What about?" and nodded for him to take a seat.

As he was seated, he introduced himself as Reuben McNutt. "I've got a few claims in the area, and I was wondering what you are going to do with the claim your family has up West Fork?"

"Well, I, uh, I don't rightly know. It's a good claim and showing good color, but I don't think I could work it by myself. I haven't thought about it much."

"Oh, I understand, and I don't mean to take advantage of you at all. I have several other claims and I was just thinking it might be of help to you to sell it and have the ready cash for whatever you need to do. I know it must be hard having lost your family and such, and this town will probably be under several feet of snow in a few weeks and that just makes things worse." He paused, looked from Ema to Cord and asked, "What do you think, Marshal? You think it'd be good for her to sell and start over somewhere else? You know, away from the memories of all that's happened and such?"

"Depends," responded Cord, "What do you think her claim is worth?"

"Dunno for sure," he began, looked at Ema and asked, "Do you have any ore samples?"

Ema grinned, turned around and dug in her pants pockets and brought out a small poke and sat it on the table proudly. "That's from me'n Everett workin' two days!"

McNutt carefully picked up the poke, poured some of the granules out and a good-sized nugget fell into his palm and his eyes flared, his eyebrows lifted, and he looked wide-eyed at Ema and back at the gold in his palm. "That is good!" He sifted the gold around in his palm, looked at her and back at the gold and began calculating in his mind and frowned, looked at Ema and said, "I'll give you twenty-five hundred dollars for the claim!"

Cord glanced at Ema, back to McNutt, and back to Ema. She sat stoic, eyes squinting, obviously mentally calculating what she thought and what her brother had talked about, and then looked at McNutt. "I think it's worth more than that, but since winter's comin' and I wanna leave, I'll take an even three thousand dollars."

McNutt frowned, looked at the gold again, took a deep breath and said, "I'm taking a chance, but I want to help you after all you've been through, so, I agree." He extended his hand to shake on the agreement and added, "I will give you a draft on our bank that you can cash at any bank you come to, will that be alright?"

Ema frowned, looked at Cord who nodded

slightly, and smiled as she shook hands with McNutt and replied, "That will be fine, Mr. McNutt!"

She turned to Cord, "Will you take me outta here?"

Cord grinned, "Oh, I s'pose I can do that, but we might end up makin' a few stops along the way, but we'll get wherever you wanna go."

Ema smiled and watched as Andy brought the plates of food for the three. She looked back at Cord, "Can we leave today?"

"Ummhmm, planned on it!" he answered and pulled his plate closer.

21

FRIENDS

WITH ANIMAS FORKS BEHIND THEM, THE TRAIL THEY RODE followed the Animas River southward. The cold air of early winter pushed them along the trail as they savored the beauty of the mountain valley. On their right, the spear-tipped fir gathered together to climb the hillside that garnered the sunlight and stored it for the coming winter. On the left, bald talus slopes rose steeply to meet the rugged escarpments that hung menacingly high above the trail. Before them, granite-tipped mountain peaks basked in the early snow that clung to the steep slopes, contrasting the brilliant white with the crystalline blue of the cloudless sky while off their left shoulder, the sun was beginning to fade and the shadows were beginning to stretch across the narrow canyon. Beside them, the Animas River giggled its way south between ice-crusted banks that were laden with kinnikinnick, currant, and willow bushes, all with sparkling icicles hanging from the remaining fall colors of red, orange, and yellow leaves. It had turned into a beautiful day and Cord breathed deep of the clear mountain air, glanced to his side to see the almost frail appearing Emaline who hunkered into the heavy collar of her woolen winter coat.

"We should make Boullion City before dark, maybe further," he paused, shrugged, "we can stop anytime and put on some coffee and some venison strip steak. I've still got a little of that left," shared Cord, glancing to Emaline.

With the collar raised, Cord could not see her face, but she answered, "You don't hafta stop on my account. I'm fine! Whenever you get hungry, we can stop an' I'll do the cookin'."

Cord grinned, wondering just how old she was, because sometimes she looked and sounded like a little girl in her teens, and other times more like a mature, though petite, woman. He did not bring her along to cook for him, but if she insisted, he would willingly oblige. But the reason they were together was to get her to Saguache and the stage line. She had said the only family she had was back east somewhere and he had assumed she wanted to return to what most called civilization. Although after her display of vengeance back at Animas Forks when she caught up with Bull and company had shown him she was more than capable of taking care of herself, but...still, this was the wilderness and men outnumbered women more than a hundred to one.

And there was something about that girl that stirred Cord's interest, he wasn't quite sure what, but something.

When they came to Grouse Gulch, the trail, or road, such as it was, crossed to the west bank of the Animas River and the crossing over the icy banks and icy water was a bit perilous, but the horses and mule were anxious to cross and made it safe. Once on the far bank, the trail weaved around several rugged rocky escarpments and turned south into the yawning mouth of the steep-sided canyon. But even in the canyon, the steep walls showed prospect holes where gold hunters had sought their treasure and failed.

The clatter of hooves echoed down the canyon before them and the wind, although slight, whistled the warning of their approach. Deep shadows blanketed the canyon bottom, while the beginning shades of dusk arched overhead and the remaining sunlight stretched the shadows across the higher shoulders of the mountains. The two new friends rode in silence, each savoring the beauty of God's creation and the quiet moments in their own way.

The fading light prompted Cord to look for a campsite even though they were still north of Boullion City. As they neared the mouth of Porcupine Gulch, Cord nudged Kwitcher off the trail and into the quakies. He saw the little bit of a spring-fed creek that cut through the aspen and a grassy bottomed shoulder amid the white-barked whispering quakies and nodded to Ema that this would be their camp for the night.

She let a smile split her face as she reined her Appaloosa mare nearer the trees, quickly stepped down and started stripping off her saddle. She stroked the neck of the horse, talking quietly to her new best friend that she had traded for by giving the horses of her brother and father to the smithy at Animas Forks in exchange for this horse, a newer saddle that was more her size and all the other tack she needed. It was just a little way she chose to start a new beginning without the constant memory of the horses of her brother and father. The horse, a blood bay, that had been her saddle horse, was now her pack horse and both seemed to be happier for it.

Cord had already stripped the gear from Kwitcher and the mule and stacked the cooking gear by what would be their campfire. He had gathered a couple armloads of long dead and dry firewood, and was making a fire circle for their campfire when Ema came near and asked, "Where's the meat and such so I can get started?"

Cord grinned, nodded to the nearby pack and asked, "There might be some currants and raspberries down along the creek, and I might be able to catch us some fresh trout, if you'd rather have fish instead of venison for supper?"

She looked to the sky and the fading light, felt the chill of the air and said, "Maybe some berries, but I think the venison will be good. Maybe we can stop a little earlier tomorrow or the next day and get the fish. Right now, I'm hungry and tired and would rather eat and turn in, if that's alright with you?"

They made short work of their supper and soon were sitting on the bedrolls near the fire. Ema sat cross-legged with her hands on her ankles as she stared into the flames. Cord was beside the fire, a little downhill and to the right of Ema. At Ema's request, they had lain their bedrolls so their heads would be near one another. She said she wanted to be able to easily talk with one another, but now they sat and shared. Ema frowned and pointed to Cord's rolled blanket for a pillow and asked, "Is that a Bible by your pillow?"

"It is," answered Cord, reaching for the leather-bound tome. He asked, "Have you ever read it?" holding it before him.

"Uh, no. Never had one before, but Pa talked about it some, you know when we were like this, sittin' around a fire, reminiscing and such."

"What do you know about it?" asked Cord, setting the Bible on his lap, letting it fall open.

"Uh, well, lemme see. I know there's a Heaven; that's the good place. And a Hell, and that's the bad place. There's God and Jesus, and oh yeah, somewhere there," pointing to the book, "it talks about the Ten Commandments, you know, where it tells you what'chu oughta be doin' and not doin.' You know, like no stealin', lyin', and such like." She smiled, nodding and pleased with herself. "Pa told us that much."

"Okay, there's a Heaven and Hell. Other than one being good and the other bad, you know anything else about them?"

"Uh, what else is there?" asked Ema, squirming around a little, getting more comfortable on the bedroll.

"Well, where do you want to go when you die?"

"Well, Heaven, of course. Wouldn'tchu?" she asked.

Cord chuckled, then asked, "You know how to get there? Heaven, I mean?"

Ema frowned, took a deep breath that lifted her shoulders and said, "Uh, I reckon by doin' more good than bad, ain't that right? You know, kinda balancing things out."

Cord smiled, "Well, if that's how, just how much good do we hafta do?"

"I dunno," mumbled Ema, frowning and dropping her eyes.

"May I show you?"

"Show me? How you gonna show me?" asked Ema, looking wide-eyed at Cord.

"From the Bible."

"Oh, sure. I'd like to know that, go ahead," she said, nodding to the Bible and scooting a little closer.

Cord moved closer as well, opening the Bible by the light of the campfire to show Ema the verses he wanted her to see and began with, "Here in I John

5:13, God explains, *These things have I written unto you that believe on the name of the Son of God; that ye may know that ye have eternal life, and that ye may believe on the name of the Son of God.* Eternal life, that's not just living here on earth, because we all have to die and that's not eternal. Eternal life is to live forever, and the only place we can live forever is in Heaven with God. Now, these words were written *that ye may know ye have eternal life.* Would you like me to show you how you can know, know for sure that Heaven is yours?"

Ema smiled, scooted even closer and said, "Sure! Yes, I wanna know!"

Cord also smiled and said, "Alright. Let's turn back to the book of Romans," and as he spoke he flipped the pages of the Bible to open it in the book of Romans. "Now, here in chapter three God explains, in verse 23 *For all have sinned, and come short of the glory of God.* And in verse 10 *As it is written there is none righteous, no, not one.* See Ema, what we need to understand, is that everyone, you, me, everyone, has sinned. You know, done bad things." He looked at her and with a stern frown, she nodded and motioned to the Bible for him to continue. "So, there's no one that has not sinned, none are righteous. And it all started with the first man, Adam. In chapter 5 verse 12 He says, *Wherefore, as by one man,* that's Adam, *sin entered into the world, and death by sin; and so death passed upon all men for that all have sinned.* Then He also says, in chapter 3 verse 23, *For all have sinned and come short of the glory of God.* And in Chapter 6 verse 23 *For the wages of sin is death*...He reminds us that we have all sinned but He goes on to say because of our sin, we've *come short* or missed out on Heaven or *the glory of God,* and that same sin draws wages which is death. Now that's not just dying and going to the grave, that is eternal punishment and eternity in Hell. That's what we deserve as sinners. But..." he paused, smiling as he turned the pages, "He continues in verse 23, *but the gift of God is eternal life through Jesus Christ our Lord."*

"See, there's that *eternal life* again, but notice, it is *the gift of God.* See, God makes it possible for us to know for sure that Heaven is our home. He offers us the gift of God, which is eternal life in Heaven, and like any gift, He also tells us how it can be ours. In Romans chapter 10 verse 9 *That if thou shalt confess with thy mouth the Lord Jesus and shalt believe in thine heart that God hath raised him from the dead, thou shalt be saved. For with the heart man believeth unto righteousness; and with the mouth confession is made unto salvation.* And verse 13 *For whosoever shall call upon the name of the Lord shall be saved.*

"See, it's that simple. We're sinners, the penalty for sin is death and hell forever, but Christ paid the penalty, or paid the bill. But for it to be ours, we have to ask for that gift of the paid bill or salvation so we will be saved from that eternity in hell and given the gift of Heaven forever. Do you understand that, Ema?"

She sat stoically, thinking, and slowly nodded. "Yes, yes. I understand. So, all I have to do is ask for that gift and it's mine?"

Cord slowly smiled, "Yes. It's that simple. And if you want, I'll lead us in prayer for you to do that. Is that what you'd like?"

"Ummhmm, please." She answered almost in a whisper and bowed her head and waited.

Cord began the simple prayer with "Our Father in heaven, we come to you to ask for that gift of eternal life..." he continued with the simple statement that Ema repeated that she knew she was a sinner and that Christ paid the penalty for her sin. She asked for forgiveness for that sin and for Christ to come into her heart and give her that gift of eternal life and together they said, "Amen!"

Ema looked up, a broad smile on her face, and looked at Cord, "Oh, thank you! Thank you! I've wondered about that a long time, but I had no one to tell me. Thank you."

Cord nodded and said, "My privilege, thank you."

They both were quiet as they watched the fire die down but the air was cool and Cord gathered a couple armloads of firewood, dropped it beside the fire and sat down on the bedroll and they crawled into their blankets. Cord kept his rifle under the blanket with him, and his pistol in the holster at his head, but he trusted Blue and Kwitcher to do as always, be vigilant through the night and he trusted his faithful friends who had never failed him.

22

SOLDIERS

Cord was awakened by big lacy snowflakes that drifted down and landed lightly on his face. The cold stirred him to wakefulness and he frowned as he looked up to see nothing but the white of snowflakes all about. He hunkered into his blankets and stretched out to grab some more firewood to stir the fire awake. When the flames licked at the dry wood, Cord glanced to Ema who had covered her head with the blanket and lay unmoving. He grinned, chuckled a little, and did the same.

When he woke, it was the weight of snow on his blanket that brought him awake. He flipped the heavy blanket back and icy snowflakes found their way to every exposed portion of flesh, and he felt it mostly on his neck, making him scrunch into his shoulders and try to get the cold and wet flakes away. He stood, looking around at the heavy white blanket that covered the ground, hung heavy on the fir and spruce, but had been mostly shed by the aspen that still held stubbornly to their golden leaves. It was quiet, a stillness that can only be found in the high country after the first big snowstorm. The heavy blanket of cottony white muffled any sound and brought a stillness and peace to the deep valley that lay between the towering mountains that were now crowned with white.

It was cold, but not the bitter cold that is often found in the high country. It was as if the blanket of white added a layer of comfort to the countryside. Cord stirred up the fire, dug out the frying pan and put some bacon in the pan, then put the coffee pot on the rock beside the fire. The lid open and snow melting in the pot. After setting the Dutch oven beside the fire, he busied himself with fashioning some biscuits that filled the Dutch oven. He replaced the lid and covered the lid with hot coals, finagled it into place with sticks of firewood. He heard a muffled mumble from the bedroll of Ema and he chuckled as he said, "You gonna sleep all day?"

"It's cold! An' I'm covered with snow!"

"Ummhmm, but I got breakfast cookin' an' we need to get a move on 'fore another storm rolls in and we get stuck here all winter!" declared Cord, grinning at the mumbling of Ema, making sounds like a newborn kitten as she complained, refusing to come from under the blankets.

"Wake me when it's ready! I ain't comin' out till I haf'ta."

The sun had risen but refused to show its face, staying hidden behind the snow-capped peaks of the San Juan mountain range. Cord looked to the shadowy but white crested peaks and calculated it would be mid-morning or later before any direct sunlight touched the bottom of the valley of the Animas. But they had to be well on their way by that time. He nudged Emaline with the toe of his boot, "Hey girl, it's 'haf'ta' time! We need to have breakfast and get on the trail!"

Mumbling and grumbling the girl threw off the blanket, fluffed the snow from her hair and jammed her hat down as she stumbled to her feet, looking around. She paused as she looked at the shimmering gold of the aspen that were shedding the last of the snow, at the white blanket that still hugged the pines, and the stillness of the valley. She smiled and looked at Cord and whispered, "It's beautiful!"

Cord grinned and chuckled, "Ummhmm. It sure is! But I'm hungry, how 'bout you?"

"Yes!" she emphatically declared as she dropped into a crouch and with a stick lifted the lid of the Dutch oven. "Mmmm, you're a good cook! I might hafta keep you around!" she giggled.

It was a light snow, big flakes that lay like downy cotton, and a little over six inches deep, but as the day began to warm, the snow settled and slid from the golden leaves of the aspen, but hugged tightly to the fir and spruce whose branches hung humbly under the fresh snow. The trail sided the river, but the slopes were bright with the white of snow and the gold of the aspen and they had traveled less than a mile when the wide maw of Cunningham Gulch let the sunlight dance on the crystalline snowflakes. But it was a brief glimpse of brightness as the shadows of the mountains stood tall with the black timber that fought to free itself of the new snow but the sun would not reach those slopes till midday and Cord and Ema would be well past.

They rode in silence, enjoying the quiet of the fresh snowfall, but the sudden scream and whistle of a camp-robber jay startled Ema who jumped in her saddle and looked about, "I thought all birds went south for the winter! What's that?"

Cord chuckled, "That's a camp-robber jay. They hide food for the winter and stick around. All those different calls, the chirp-chirp, the screaming whistle, that's all jays!"

He nodded to a half-naked aspen, "There's one on that bare branch of the aspen yonder."

"Well, I'd seen 'em before, but I din't know they stayed the winter."

"Didn't you and your brother stay last winter?" asked Cord, frowning.

"No! We left early. Pa had him another claim by the Rio Grande down there where it comes outta the mountains. He had him a cabin we stayed in with him. It was his partner's and his, but the partner left an' went back home to Pennsylvania."

"Was the claim any good?"

"Nah, but the cabin was, so..." she shrugged and fell quiet and pensive, remembering her father and brother.

"You never did say where you had family and where you were going," started Cord, wondering just what she had in mind. But the trail neared the edge of the river and the crashing of white water ended any possibility of conversation, at least for a while. As they rounded the point of the talus slope that fell from the high mountains on the northwest side, they broke into the wider valley where the river was fed by Soda Gulch and further on by Mineral Creek. It was a valley that was just a little shy of a mile wide and a couple miles long.

And like everywhere else, the hillsides were freckled with prospect holes and miners' tents that sided the river, but what caught Cord's attention was the orderly formation of smaller canvas shelters that told of the presence of an army unit. He frowned at the presence of troops but quickly realized the only reason for them being in the high country would probably be because of the Ute people led by Chief Ouray. He shook his head at the thought of any conflict, especially after being in on the treaty negotiations that took place earlier in the summer.

He reined up, looked over at Ema and said, "There might be trouble brewing." He began to explain about the treaty that had become known as the Brunot Agreement, and that it called for the Ute people to move out of the area and go to the designated reservation further south. "I'm guessing the soldiers are here to make sure the Ute go south, but, unless I miss my guess, there's gonna be trouble. I think they," nodding toward the encampment of soldiers, "are the 9th Cavalry out of Fort Garland under Major Hatch. I've dealt with them before. The troopers are good men, but sometimes the leadership lacks a little. You see, they're called Buffalo Soldiers by the Ute people, that's because they're all coloreds, most veterans of the recent conflict between the states, and the leaders are all Whites. Don't ask me why, I know it doesn't make any sense, but that's the way of the army sometimes."

He nudged Kwitcher on the trail to pass by the army encampment, Ema staying alongside. Cord remembered the Ute often camped up Mineral Creek west of the flats. He thought it would be good if he stopped by their camp, just to get a feel of what was in the air. He shook his head at the thought of another conflict, he had many friends among the Tabeguache Ute and the Uncompahgre Ute, the two branches of the Ute people that were led by Chief Ouray.

As they turned their backs on the wide valley and started up the canyon of Mineral Creek, huge escarpments of red oxide colored stone loomed over the trail, and higher up the mountainside, more stood menacingly over the long talus slope that fell from high up, showing the remains of other rocky escarpments that fell to the erosion of mountain weather.

Across the creek, that now showed mostly ice with icicles dangling from the overhanging branches of streamside willows and alders, on the south side of the narrow canyon, steep timber-covered slopes rose steadily under the snow-burdened pines, thrusting the peak of Sultan Mountain into the cloudy sky high above.

In a short distance, the widening valley of Mineral Creek showed the tipi tops of the encampment of the Ute people. Cord and Ema no sooner came from the mouth of the canyon than they were confronted by a group of warriors, probably Warriors of the Wolf, that were the guardians of the people. There were eight of the stoic faced warriors that sat their horses, blocking the trail, until one of the warriors kneed his mount forward and he lifted his lance high, stopping Cord and Ema. Cord lifted his right hand and greeted the warriors in the tongue of the Ute, "Maykw(a)".

The warrior returned the greeting, then spoke in English, "It is good to see our brother, Cordell. Why do you come to our village?"

"And it is good to see you, Standing Elk. We come at the invitation of Chief Ouray and our many friends among the people."

"Follow us," demanded Standing Elk, without awaiting a response. He reined his mount around, motioning to the others, and without a glance back to Cord, started toward the center of the village. Most villages were arranged so the chief's lodge would be the center of the village, and easily identifiable by the size and the banners that flew from the tipi poles. It was easy to spot the lodge, and Cord also noticed the lodge of the Medicine Man that was painted in a similar fashion, had ribbons at the poles, and was also located near the center of the village. He smiled at the memory of Lone Eagle, the beautiful woman who held the position of Medicine Man, or woman, and also called the Shaman.

Cord followed Standing Elk, motioning for Ema to stay close and as they rode through the village, Cord softly spoke to Ema, explaining his connection to the people and why they were welcomed and he was recognized. He also explained a little about the relationship with Lone Eagle, and grinned at the reaction of Ema as she giggled and ducked her head, hiding her face from Cord.

23

FRIENDS

THEY GATHERED NEAR THE LODGE OF CHIEF OURAY. Broken Arrow, his sister, Lone Eagle, and Chipeta, Ouray's wife were seated in a semi-circle apart from the cookfire that was tended by two women of the village. When Cord and Ema came near, Ouray greeted them, motioned for them to be seated to his left and Cord nodded, but before being seated, Cord introduced Ema. "Chief Ouray, Chipeta, Lone Eagle, Broken Arrow, this," he said, turning to motion to Ema, "Is Emaline Appleby. Her family had a mining claim up near the forks of the Animas, but her father and brother were murdered by the outlaws. I am taking her to Saguache to catch a stage back to family, back east." The others nodded to Ema, and Cord seated himself as he motioned for Ema to be seated to his left. Ouray was on his right and the others beyond Ouray. As soon as Cord and Ema were seated, the women started serving the meal, carrying wood platters loaded with food to each one.

Cord turned to Ouray, "I was surprised to see your people still camped here. I thought you would have already gone to the reservation. Why do you wait?"

Ouray nodded, let a slow grin split his face as he accepted a platter from one of the women, then turned to Cord, "We leave with the coming of the sun."

"How long have the soldiers been here?" asked Cord, also accepting a platter of food.

"They came at the end of day, this will be their first day here," replied Ouray.

Cord nodded, began to eat his meal. Among the native peoples, it was not the custom for meals to be interrupted by conversation, but Cord and these leaders of the people had been together many times and they had become accustomed to using the time of meals to speak of important issues.

At a pause in the serving, Ouray looked at Cord, "I can see our brother is bothered by the coming of the soldiers. Do not let it trouble you. We will go as we said and there is no need for them to be here. We had to hunt for our winter meat. The land where we go, what you call the reservation, does not have the elk of the high country and our people must be prepared."

"Has Colonel Hatch called on you yet?" asked Cord, referring to the commandant of the 9th Calvary.

"No. He may visit yet this day," offered Chief Ouray, looking at the sun high in the sky and giving a warmth to the wintry day. The snow was melting and the creeks were flowing high and this promised to be a much better day for traveling. Cord was anxious to get on the trail, but he wanted assurance from both Ouray and Hatch that there would be no conflict between forces.

Broken Arrow interjected, "We do have two groups of hunters that have yet to return. We wait for them, and the women that must prepare the meat for our travel will be ready, but it may take another day." Arrow glanced to Ouray, noticed his expression and knew he was not pleased with Arrow's remarks. Broken Arrow added, "But some of that work can be done on the trail."

Cord asked, "I know the meat must be cut up to dry, and when you make the pemmican, there are berries and such that are added. Surely that cannot be done on the move, can it?"

Broken Arrow looked to his sister, Lone Eagle, and she explained, "It is not done on the move, as you put it, but it can be done when we make camp for the night. We use much of the fresh meat for food on the journey, but if we must take an extra day or so, why can we not do that?"

Cord dropped his eyes; the nearness of this woman always stirred him. They had almost joined in marriage, but because of their individual responsibilities, hers as a shaman, Cord's as a marshal, they were prevented from joining. But the love and respect for one another was still there, and like most couples, it is hard to say no to one another. Yet Cord glanced to the chief, then to Broken Arrow, and explained, "I will talk to Colonel Hatch. Perhaps I can get him to allow you more time for the preparation of the meat. But I cannot make promises for him."

Ouray let a slow grin tug at the corners of his mouth as he looked from Cord to Lone Eagle, for he knew of their affection, but he sobered his expression as he said, "The elk do not have the timetable, but we must have the meat. The colonel is a leader of men and will understand the way of the hunter."

"Let's hope so. The last thing we need is some kind of conflict between the people and the soldiers," surmised Cord, finishing the last of his food and setting the platter aside.

Broken Arrow also set his platter aside but added, "If there is conflict, our people will not start it." It was more of a pronouncement than a platitude, but Cord understood. The Ute had given up much to have peace, signing over more than three and a half million acres of the mountain country with all the game they were accustomed to hunting, and receiving a small portion of land with minimal game and a stipend of less than thirty thousand dollars per year. Although they were to be allowed to continue to hunt in their homelands, they could not live there. Many gold hunters had already come into the mountains and more would be expected in the spring, their presence making the hunting difficult and conflict between the people and the miners would certainly occur.

After they finished their meal, Cord and Ema left the encampment and rode west down Mineral Creek, the trail taking them to the mouth of the wide gulch that was sided by the San Juan mountains, those on the north side showing long and steep talus slopes that showed the dusty yellow and umber colors of iron ore, while on the south side, black timber, some still holding on to the fresh snow, climbed the steep rocky slopes toward the high peaks that scraped the blue of the afternoon sky.

When they came from the mouth of the gulch, they were on high ground and less than two miles up the Animas River, the canvas coverlets of the Buffalo Soldiers blossomed on the grassy bank. Cord reined up, leaned forward on the pommel of his saddle and looked from the encampment to Ema and explained, "I'm gonna hafta go there to talk to the soldiers. If I don't, they just might get a little anxious and start something with Ouray and his people. Can't have that!"

"I understand. Let's go if we're goin', cuz the day ain't gettin' any longer!" she grinned, nodding toward the encampment.

Cord grinned, nodded, and nudged Kwitcher onto the trail that lay in the shadows of the lower Aspen that fluttered in the breeze, having shed the morning snow. He led the way, with Blue out front,

Kwitcher taking a quick step, and the mule tugging at the lead rope. Ema followed with her pack horse behind and the small entourage caught the eye of some of the miners that were working on building log cabins in anticipation of the coming winter. There were a handful of cabins underway, scattered cabins and a few skeletons of what would probably become stores or some other commercial building that would soon make up another town.

Although known only as Baker's Park, Cord knew this would probably grow into a town. He had heard the names of some early miners like William Kearnes, Dempsey Reese and Thomas Blair, as men that were considering developing the area, building a town, businesses, and ore processing stamp mills and more, but only time would tell how and how soon all that would happen. Right now, Cord was only interested in keeping the peace between the influx of gold-hungry miners and the people of the Ute nation.

As they neared the bivouac area a husky soldier stepped out on the trail and stopped them with a "Halt! Who goes there?" as he stood in the middle of the trail, a rifle held diagonally across his chest and a frown on his face.

Cord reined up, called Blue back, and answered, "I'm Marshal Cordell Beckett. I'd like to see Colonel Hatch."

"And jus' what is yo' bizness?"

Cord grinned, pushed his hat back away from his

brow and looked at the soldier who was big, scowling with a wrinkled brow, and whose hat was pinned up on the left side with a turkey feather, and the buttons on his uniform were protesting the tight fight across the big chested man. Cord answered, "I want to talk to him about the Tabeguache and Uncompahgre Ute people that are camped up the Mineral Gulch. We need to discuss the Brunot Agreement and the conditions of the Ute hunting."

The man frowned, nodded, and said, "Wait-chere!" and turned on his heel and went to the colonel's tent, the largest in the encampment, to give his report. Within moments, the man returned and said as he pointed to the tent, "You can go to the colonel's quarters. I'll take your horses."

Cord nodded and swung down, motioning Ema to do the same and come with him, leaving the four animals in the care of the soldier, who appeared a little exasperated with the task. Cord spoke to Blue, "Stay with the horses!" and motioned him to the ground. The dog hung his head, dropped to the ground beside Kwitcher and watched Cord and Ema walk through the camp to go to the Colonel's tent.

"Well, good afternoon Marshal! And who do we have here?" questioned the colonel, standing and smiling at Ema and extending his hand in greeting. Cord noticed the colonel's attention to Ema and chose to file it away in his mind and turned his attention to the present predicament. Cord responded with the introduction, "Colonel Hatch, this is

Emaline Appleby. Ema, this is Colonel Hatch of the 9th Cavalry out of Fort Union and Fort Garland."

The colonel glanced at Cord with a questioning frown, but focused his attention on the young woman before him and accepted her hand, gave a bit of a bow and nod, motioned both to be seated and seated himself apart from and facing them. He looked at Cord and asked, "And to what do I owe this visit, Marshal?"

"We just came from the encampment of the Ute and a short visit with Chief Ouray. Seeing your camp, I was a little concerned as to your presence here. *Is* there a particular reason for you and your troops to be here, Colonel?"

"Of course. We don't do anything without purpose. We are the cavalry after all." His answer was a bit gruff and came from a frowning face as the Colonel focused his attention on the marshal.

"And that purpose is…?" asked Cord.

The colonel scooted to the edge of his seat, put his elbows on his knees and leaned forward as he glared at Cord to begin his answer. "First off, I am not in the habit of telling civilians anything regarding our purpose and orders. But in this case, I'll explain. We are here to ensure the Ute people leave this area and to escort them to the reservation, since this is no longer their land, and we will do so in accordance with the recent signed treaty executed at the Los Piños Agency. We will escort the entire tribe beginning tomorrow at sunrise."

Cord dropped his head, shaking it slowly side to side and lifted his eyes to the colonel. "First off, Colonel, that was *not* a treaty that was signed at Los Piños—it was an agreement in principle! Yes, they surrendered the land as their home, however, they reserved the right to hunt all this land at any time they choose—which is exactly what they are doing! They have to stockpile their winter supply of meat before going to the reservation! And if you expect to escort them—you best expect a fight! A fight you probably cannot win!" Cord growled the last statement and gave just as stern an expression to his manner as did the colonel.

The colonel came to his feet and began shaking his finger at Cord, who remained seated. "How dare you imply that my troops could not win a fight against these heathen redskins! My men are experienced troopers and could whip any band of these... these..." he stumbled as he tried to find a derogatory term for the Ute warriors, but Cord quickly offered an answer.

"These are experienced warriors—every one of them! And they are probably better armed than your cavalry—what is it *they* carry, the Springfield carbine? These warriors—most of them already have either the Spencer repeater or the Winchester repeaters! And every one of their warriors are what you call 'blooded' in battle! They have been fighting since they were big enough to pull a bowstring! By the way, what do you have, fifty, sixty troopers?

Broken Arrow, the leader of their warrior society, has over one hundred warriors—all better armed and all experienced! And if there's a fight, the first thing they do is send word to every other band and within a day, there will be several hundred more warriors on their way here!"

The colonel's eyes grew wide at that revelation and he sat back down, looking around the tent, fuming in his anger, but he looked up at Cord, "What about the treaty? They said they would willingly go to the reservation!?"

"And they are willing. They are waiting for the last of their hunting parties to return, take a day or so to prepare the meat, and they will take to the trail to go to the reservation. And remember, Colonel, they are not breaking a treaty—that is not a treaty, it is an agreement. A treaty has to be ratified by congress, this is just an agreement, which they are willing to abide by and will. They reserved their hunting rights and that's all they are doing. If you start a fight, you're going to lose some good men unnecessarily." Cord paused, took a deep breath, and continued, "Now, Colonel, I was at Los Piños, and served as an interpreter for Ouray and the other chiefs. If you do this, try to force them to go before they are ready, not only will you be going against the agreement and this band of Ute, the word will quickly spread and every Ute band that was present at the Brunot signing, will rise up and go to war against every White man, every prospector, every town, every farmer, in the western half of Colorado territory. And that won't be a pretty sight, believe me."

The colonel continued to fume and fumble around, suddenly coming to his feet and stomping around as he glared at Cord and said, "I don't take my orders from you! You have no authority over me—and I'm not going to let some back country uneducated badge packer try making my decisions for me! I am responsible for this territory, not you!" He stepped closer to Cord, hovered over him and began shaking his finger at him as he continued, "And I will do what I think is best, in accordance with the orders I have received. I take my orders from General Sheridan and *only* General Sheridan! He said to get these Indians out of here before the miners start shootin' 'em! His words! And if we have to shoot them first—that's exactly what we will do!"

Cord stood and faced the colonel and with his head slightly tilted, he growled his response, "Be assured, Colonel—you do not have the authority to restrain me, but uniform or no uniform, *I* have the authority to arrest you, if necessary. But when I leave here, I will go immediately to the nearest telegraph office and send word to both Governor McCook and Felix Brunot about your utter disregard for the agreement they made with the Ute people and that any loss of life, whether Ute or White or soldier, will be totally on your shoulders!" With a nod to Ema, she rose and the two left the colonel's tent.

24
STANDOFF

Cord and Ema mounted up and started off downstream of the Animas, keeping to the well-traveled trail. But when a bend in the river put them out of sight of the soldier's encampment, Cord turned back to the north, taking the trail that sided Mineral Creek and would take them to the Ute village. He was not surprised when they had just entered the mouth of Mineral Gulch that he was hailed and stopped by Broken Arrow and three of his warriors that were with him. "I see you have been to the soldier camp."

Cord grinned, nodding, and swung to the ground, motioning for Broken Arrow to join him on the creek bank, away from the others. The two old friends walked in silence to the edge of the creek and sat down side by side. Cord said, "It has been a long time since we have hunted together."

"Yes, you should come with us to the place of our

winter camp, the place the whites call *Reservation* and we can hunt together," responded Broken Arrow.

Cord sobered, looked at the chuckling waters of the shallow mineral creek where ice had formed around the edges and water had splashed on overhanging branches that were now heavy with long icicles. "There might be a problem, but it is a problem you must handle carefully." Cord faced Broken Arrow and went on to explain in detail what could happen with the over-anxious Colonel Hatch. "But if you can stop him, without a fight, you could give your people the extra time they need to prepare for the journey and keep anyone from getting killed." Cord looked around at the nearby terrain where a high finger ridge from the west bank pushed into the creek with its rocky bluffs, and behind them on the east side, steep hillsides with a long talus slope offered another long shoulder that pushed toward the creek, nudging the only trail that sided the creek closer to water's edge. Cord grinned, "And this might be the best place to have that 'talk'."

Both men stood, looked around, talked a little more, and with broad grins, the two friends clasped forearms and Cord mounted up, took the lead of his mule and with a nod to Ema, turned away from the gulch and started back toward the Animas River and the trail that would take them south and out of the high country. Cord's ultimate destination was to be Saguache for Ema to catch a stage east, but that was well over a week's travel away. He was not about to leave this area while the powder keg still had a short fuse. He just wanted to find a good campsite and a promontory that would afford him a view of the coming confrontation.

THE CAMPSITE CHOSEN by Cord was on the flanks of mountains that rose high above the valley and pierced the blue of the sky with their hoary heads of granite that stood proudly above timberline. From the peak, a long trough that often carried avalanches in the deep of winter or even early spring, now carried a trickle of water that was the snowmelt from the early snows, but offered ample water for their horses and camp needs. Their camp was tucked back in the aspen that still held tightly to their golden leaves and offered ample cover for Cord and Ema. The low shoulder of the mountain stood no more than a thousand feet above the valley floor and was directly across from the mouth of Mineral Creek gulch, where Cord knew the soldiers would have to go to approach the Ute encampment. At this point it was less than a mile to the mouth of the gulch and Cord had a clear view of the layout of the trail and creek.

He had left Ema at the camp while he led the animals to the little creek for water and soon returned to picket them on the grassy clearing atop the shoulder. Once the animals were secured, Cord ambled into camp to see Ema busy at the cookfire preparing their supper. "What's for supper?" he asked as he found himself a seat on a nearby rock.

Ema smiled and looked over her shoulder at Cord, "Oh, just makin' do with the leftovers you been packin' around. 'Course I had to find somethin' to go with 'em and make 'em taste a mite better, but I think it'll do."

Cord chuckled, "Well, it smells powerful good. I'm so hungry my belly button's pinchin' muh backbone!"

Ema giggled, "Oh, go on with you! Seems like ever' time I look atchu, you're eatin' on sumpin'."

"Wal, I learned a long time ago that when you're travelin' in wild country and you get a chance to eat, best do it, cuz you never know when you might get another meal."

"Well, this here's a good meal. We got venison steaks wrapped in bacon, Indian potatoes with carrots, biscuit root and cattail root. For dessert, I made us up a batch of berries to go with the biscuits, what muh momma used to call strawberry shortcake, but this has other berries too."

"Where'd you get all that?"

"Whenever we stopped somewhere, you might remember I'd usually go for a little walk, lookin' around and would come back with muh pockets full!"

"You're mighty handy to have around!" Cord chuckled, then added, "Well, let's get to eatin', muh mouth's waterin' already!"

"Then you best be sayin' a prayer to thank God for this food, don'chu think?" Ema giggled, smiling at Cord.

"So, do you think the soldiers are gonna go against the Ute people?" asked Ema. They sat near one another on the big slab of rock they had used for a table but now shared it as a bench as they looked at the glowing embers of the fire. Supper and its clean-up was behind them, and they both clasped hot cups of coffee, enjoying the night sounds and the distant howl of coyotes that rose above the treetops.

"I think they might. That colonel is determined to have his way and like many that have the authority over others, they think they're right and they have a hard time admitting that sometimes it's better to be cautious rather than right. But I think Broken Arrow will do his best to keep anything bad from happening. All we can do is wait and see." Cord took a long sip of his hot coffee and glanced to Ema, appreciating the way the firelight and moonlight lit her face. He thought she was a very pretty young woman and was proving herself to be more woman than the little sister he first thought.

"So, this family you have back east, are they close relatives?" asked Cord.

"Dunno, I mean I don't know them very well. Only heard Pa talk about 'em, never met 'em. The woman is the sister of my mother, and she has a family of three or four young'uns. They live in Kentucky, some place on the river called Paducah. Her husband is a captain on one o' them steamboats on the river. Leastways, that's what Pa said. Pa's family had a farm near Cape Girardeau, Missouri. He ran off when he was big 'nuff, went to Independence, met Ma, got married then joined the army for the war, an' somewhere along there, me'n muh brother joined 'em." She grinned and giggled at the memory of the family.

"But we left Missouri right after the war, to come west and start a new life. Ma died on the wagon train, an' the only thing Pa wanted to do was go to the mountains and find some gold." She shrugged, picked up a stick and tossed it at the hot coals, lapsing into deep thought and memories.

"So, you don't really know where you're going when you catch a stage, do you?" asked Cord.

"Nope!" she answered, staring at the low-burning fire as it began to consume the stick.

They sat in silence for a while until Cord suggested, "We better turn in and get some sleep. Blue and the horses will warn us if anything gets near so we should sleep alright. If anything is going to happen between the soldiers and the Ute, it'll probably be right about sunup. So...I reckon we oughta get some sleep." He rose and walked to the bedrolls and stretched out on the blankets, lying for a while with his hands cupped behind his head as he admired the clear starlit sky above.

THE RISING sun was just beginning to tint the snow-capped peaks on the west side of the valley in shades of pink and pale orange. The long shadows from the mountains on the east edge of the valley stretched across the bottom like a dark cold blanket, that was slowly receding as the sun began to show its face. Cord had risen before first light and spent his time with the Lord, concerned about the coming confrontation and the uncertainty of the journey of Ema. But now he lay prostrate across a wide boulder, his blanket beneath him, and his binoculars before him. He had heard the sounds of the awakening troops and they were just beginning to move out from their camp.

Cord had already seen movement among the trees that sided Mineral Creek at the mouth of the gulch and knew Broken Arrow and the Warriors of the Wolf had already taken position to safeguard their people. He muttered another simple prayer, *Lord, how bout'chu standing between these two forces, keep 'em from killin' each other?* He took a deep breath and focused the field glasses on the trail that would be taken by the soldiers. The oft-used trail was a two-track trail used by prospectors with their two-wheeled carts and wagons and by the Uncompahgre Ute dragging their travois to their hunting camp.

Cord watched as the usual formation of the troops rode two abreast, the scouts out front and the officers at the head of the columns. As he watched, the scouts reined up, swung their mounts around and returned to face the colonel. Cord could imagine the report of their sighting movement that was probably the natives and was pleased to see the guidon bearer lower the banner of the company insignia and replace it with a white flag. The colonel, another officer, one of the scouts, and the guidon bearer rode forward and were met in the roadway by Broken Arrow and three of his warriors. At this distance, Cord could not make out who the others were, but he grinned as he watched the animated exchange.

Broken Arrow was an impressive figure with his bone hair pipe breastplate, the beaded armbands and headband, the multiple notched and colored eagle feathers at the back of his head and his buckskin leggings and moccasins, both beaded and fringed. His stern expression showed no mercy and as he spoke it was almost a growl. "You will go no further. My people are camped in this valley. We make ready to leave."

The colonel paused before he spoke, gathering himself and forcing himself to remain calm. He did not like what he perceived as belligerence on the part of this Indian before him, but he also knew he best show caution. "You will leave now, or we will make you leave!" he declared. But was taken aback as he watched the warrior before him. This man was not afraid but grinned as he looked past the colonel as if counting the troops behind him.

Broken Arrow said again, "You will go no further. If you do not stop, many will die. You have Buffalo Soldiers. We know these soldiers. They are good warriors. But we have many more men who are also good warriors. For each man you have, we have two or three. If you want to fight, we will show no mercy and will kill all. We protect our people, you protect no one."

"My soldiers are battle proven! They know how to fight and will do so if I command them."

"Why would you do that?" asked Broken Arrow as he lifted his rifle, one-handed to hold it high overhead.

When Broken Arrow dropped his arm, the mountainsides exploded with war cries, ear-shattering screams, and soaring high overhead were arrows with bone hair-pipe whistles arching across the sky, whistles screaming and ribbons trailing. The natural contours and cliffs of the mouth of the canyon made a megaphone of the terrain, magnifying the sounds and echoing the screams. The more than a hundred warriors concealed in the trees and brush on the hillsides unanimously screamed their war cries that were blood-curdling and frightful all while waving colorful feathered lances and beating on the drums, rattling the gourds and other noise makers. The frightful cacophony of the screams and sudden movements startled everything and everyone and more and accomplished the purpose of Broken Arrow and his leaders.

The men and horses of the 9th were startled and frightened at the unexpected screams. They had been led to believe the natives would cower in fear or run in fright, but these were far from fearful. They shouted and screamed their war cries, and the distracting sudden movements and colors, added to the melee and the uniformed soldiers showed white eyed fear as did their horses. The animals bolted, bucked, screamed, ducked their heads between their hooves, broke in the middle and kicked heels high, some twisting in the air, doing anything to escape the pandemonium and the control of their riders. Many blue uniformed men suddenly took flight as they valiantly fought to keep their seats and control of the horses but failed, and for most it was a losing battle. As the mounts contorted, bucked, reared up, and more to unseat their riders and escape the discordance, even the colonel and his nearby officers were not to be left out as they grabbed reins, saddle horns, handfuls of mane, and struggled to get their animals under control. The major's spirited animal reared up and pawed at the sky, twisting and appeared to be trying to climb the stairway to heaven as the major lost his grip and fell in a heap in the dirt, scrambling like a crab to get out of the way of the panicked animals.

Broken Arrow and his leaders did their best to maintain their stoic and staid attitude, but laughter took control and even though their horses were more conditioned to the turmoil about them, even they were difficult to control. But the Ute leaders quickly resumed their position on the trail, watching and witnessing something they would tell and retell around many campfires for generations to come.

The colonel, finally in control of his mount and sitting deep in his saddle held taut on the reins, looked about, and shook his head as he continued to watch the unplanned rodeo. He started to reach for his rifle, but hesitated at bringing it from the scabbard as he looked at the frowning expression of the stern warrior before him, who shook his head to stay the colonel. Hatch held his horse's head high, dug heels to the ribs of the animal, and forced him back to the trail before Broken Arrow. His junior officers also worked hard to gain control of their mounts, except for the major who was last seen chasing his horse into the aspen, waving his arms and shouting "Whoa, whoa you fool horse!" and with taut reins and firm grips on their saddles the others soon moved alongside.

The horses of the troops were scattered over the mountainsides, some tangled in the brush, others had disappeared into the aspen and pines. Those that had been caught, had to be held with tight reins, but several of the soldiers, better at marching than riding, could not control their animals as many of the spooked horses, many trembling and with wide eyes, jerked free and again took off bucking down the slope to the creek. At least three troopers took flight and went head over heels into the icy water of the creek, their horses standing spread-legged on the bank. But as many of the men began to get control of their mounts, the colonel looked at the leaders of the warriors who struggled to keep a stoic expression before the pandemonium of the troops, and scowled, forcing himself to keep his tongue.

It was obvious that they were considerably outnumbered by the many warriors obscured in the trees and rocks of the hillsides. They had not shown themselves enough for the soldiers to know how they were armed, but the colonel remembered the marshal had said most had either Spencer repeaters or Winchesters. The colonel noted that those before him all had Winchester repeater rifles.

When Broken Arrow lowered his rifle, he looked directly at the colonel and said, "Do you understand what I say?"

The colonel looked at Broken Arrow, huffed and puffed a little, then humbly asked, "Did you say your people are making ready to leave? To go to the reservation?"

"Yes. The women are preparing the meat for the journey and the rest will be ready to leave by sunup tomorrow."

The colonel looked at his junior officer, the major who had commandeered a soldier's mount, had dropped his eyes and fought to keep a straight face when all the horses had started bucking and more. The major looked at the colonel and nodded his agreement and Colonel Hatch put on his most stern expression and said, "That will be acceptable." Then in an effort to regain his composure and control, he stroked his full beard and with a stern expression, looked at Broken Arrow as he added, "But if I do not see your people on the move by this time tomorrow, we will return."

Broken Arrow nodded, and with a glance to his other warriors, the four men turned their mounts and with their backs to the soldiers, rode back up the trail. They had gone just a few yards when Broken Arrow lifted his rifle and shouted his cry of command and the hills came alive with the movement of the many warriors as they went to their horses tethered in the trees to return to the camp.

Major Dinwoody looked at Colonel Hatch and said, "They were ready for us, Colonel. It would have been a bloody mess if we pushed it!"

"Yeah," grumbled the colonel, "Now see if you can get these men back in some kind of order and let's get outta here!" as he gave the order to turn about and return to camp.

25

LONG RIDE

IN THE HIGH COUNTRY, IT TAKES A WHILE FOR THE RISING sun to bend its lances into the deep canyons, and Cord and Ema waited for full light before beginning the long ride to Saguache. Cord chose to return over the trail that would follow the Rio Grande out of the mountains of the San Juan Range. It was good country and a good trail that would also provide the possibility of getting some fresh meat. Most of the elk had already migrated to the flat lands but there were always those laggards that chose to wait and avoid the crowds, not unlike many of the men that called the high country their home.

As the sun began to show itself from behind the tall peaks with the splash of pink behind the shadowy peaks to the east, Cord was already rigging the animals, leaving only the one side of the packs on the mule open for the still perking coffee pot and the frying pan that held the last of the bacon and biscuits left over from last night.

"Why din'tchu wake me?" crowed Ema as she tossed her blankets aside and came to her feet, she had returned to her blankets after witnessing the confrontation between the Buffalo Soldiers and the Warriors of the Wolf with Broken Arrow. "I'da helped with breakfast and more if you'd just let me!" she grumbled as she ran fingers through her hair and tucked in her shirttail. She was still mumbling when she meandered into the trees for her morning habits and Cord chuckled as he finished with the packs on her horse and the saddle on her appaloosa.

"So, what're we doin' today?" she asked as she poured herself of cup of the stiff black coffee, and looked over the rim at Cord, mischief dancing in her eyes.

Cord shook his head, chuckling, and said, "We're headin' back o'er the mountains to Saguache. Wanna get there 'for the snow closes the pass. It'll be easier goin' along the Rio Grande, at least if we don't get buried with a blizzard or sumpin' like that. If we went the lowland route through the flats, it's about three days longer, and I don't know how long the stage company's gonna be runnin', what with winter comin' on."

Ema finished her coffee and grabbed up the pans and cups to finish packing the gear for the journey, but she was mumbling all the while. Cord watched her and finally asked, "So, what's all the grumblin' about?"

"Oh, I dunno. Reckon I'm not real excited about going halfway round the world to see somebody I don't even know and have no idea what I'm gonna do or what they might want. I don't even know if they'd want a orphan like me livin' with 'em."

"Orphan? Why you say that? An orphan is a youngun' that has no family, and you do! Course you ain't met 'em all, but well, you can think of me as family if you want to," suggested Cord.

"Oh?" asked Ema, smiling at Cord. "And just what kinda family are you? My father, my brother, my uncle, or...husband?" she giggled as she gave him a coy smile.

"Just family. Don't have to have no title, but if you don't like family, how 'bout friends?"

"Friends is good," laughed Ema, finishing the rigging of the pack, then added, "for now."

And they were soon on their way, heading upriver on the Animas then taking the trail that bent to the southwest and sided Cunningham Creek to Stony Gulch. Cord hoped to make it at least over Stony Pass and to the headwaters of the Rio Grande and maybe further, although this was a bit of a climb on a narrow and hazardous trail, but it was one he had traveled before and he was optimistic as to their progress for the day.

When the trail bent to the west into Stony Gulch, they crossed the path of a slab avalanche that had flattened an entire shoulder of timber, leaving behind the almost bare trunks of uniformly layered timber. The trail moved above the downed timber, crossing the steep shoulder of the mountain before crossing the gulch bottom to take to a zig-zag trail that climbed the east face of the steep walled ridge that came from the peak of Canby Mountain. The trail then bent to the south to side the dry creek bed that lay in the east–west valley between the high ridges.

The moderate climb took them about three miles in the high country before coming to the headwaters of the Rio Grande. Cord reined up, looking about the treeless terrain and feeling the icy winds of timberline. Above him to the west rose the pale yellow and grey flanks of Sheep Mountain, while below him on his right were the ash white flanks of the hills that rose above the bristlecone pines further to the west. It was the bottom of this valley that carried the shallow waters of what would eventually become the mighty Rio Grande River, but now, it was little more than a mountain creek easily stepped across by the long-legged Kwitcher. Cord looked to Ema, "There's still plenty of light, it's just a little past noon and up here we'll have more sunlight. I think we'll just go down this trail, maybe get outta the wind, and have us a bit of lunch and after that climb, the animals could use a breather."

"Suits me, and if you want to get a fire goin', I'll

get the coffee on and we'll have some biscuits and coffee! Sound good?"

"It does," chuckled Cord and nudged Kwitcher across the icy creek bed of the headwaters of the Rio Grande.

Their second day on the trail saw them following the Rio Grande into an area called Antelope Park. They had stopped at a few of the miner's claims along the way just to make themselves known and to see if there was anything happening that he should know about. One miner said, "Oh, don' know if it's anything you'd be interested in, but earlier today I had another visitor, unusual to have so many visitors this time o' year, but he was a Mex, one o' them vaqueros they call themselves. Anyway, he was askin' if we'd be needin' any horses or if'n we'd want some fresh beef. We said no on the beef, but me'n muh partner, ol' Rooster there," nodding to his busy partner who had paid little attention to their visitors, "said we might be interested in a horse or mule so we could get outta these mountains 'fore the deep snow comes. Anyway, he said he an' his friends will be comin' this way either later today or tomorrow with some horses an' such that they be glad to sell for some dust or nuggets. So..." he shrugged, grinning as he pulled on his galluses and smiled at Ema.

When the man mentioned vaqueros, Cord was reminded of those he met further south, the men that worked for John Dawson and had brought a herd of cattle from Texas to the gold fields. He knew the plan was to provide beef for the miners, but it usually was not done by bringing the live cattle to the miners and especially not the horses, for the horses were always needed to handle the cattle, and the coming of winter would be the most demanding time for horses and riders. Cord looked at the miner and asked, "Did he say how many they had, horses and cattle?"

"No, just that they had plenty for whatever we would need."

"How many vaqueros?"

"Din't ask, din't tell," answered the miner, frowning. "Why the concern?"

Cord opened his duster and vest to show his badge, "I ran into some vaqueros earlier in the summer. They were bringing in a herd for a man that was establishing his ranch down below La Loma, a new camp they're calling Del Norte, but I don't think he'd be driving horses and cattle up into the mountains at this time of year."

"Wal, they was just plannin' on sellin' 'em. I think they was wantin' some easy money, get themselves some gold dust without havin' to dig for it!" offered the miner. "But, I gotta get back to work 'fore they come back—need to get 'em some dust so we can get the horses to get outta these mountains! It's gettin' too cold for these ol' bones!" he shivered to emphasize his point.

Cord was still frowning as he dug heels to

Kwitcher's ribs to move away and back to the trail. Ema came alongside and asked, "What is it?"

Cord looked at her, chuckled, "Oh, just the lawman in me that gets suspicious too easy. Prob'ly nuthin', but something just doesn't feel right about this, this, story about the vaqueros sellin' horses and cattle."

"Didn't you say you often thought you'd like to have a cattle ranch?" asked Ema.

"Yeah. I met the man, John Dawson, when he first came into the valley. He had several vaqueros working for him as they brought up a herd of cattle from down by Santa Fe. But he wanted to get the ranch built and the cattle fattened up before they started selling anything. He said the earliest he'd be sellin' would be next spring. Now either something had changed or there is something wrong with this whole deal, and I aim to find out what's goin' on!" he declared.

He glanced over at Ema, looked at the scabbarded rifle and asked, "You any good with that?" nodding to the rifle.

Ema let a slow smile split her face as she looked coyly at Cord, "I am! That's a Winchester 1873 in .44-40, and it's a dandy! But 'fore that, I had me a Yellow Boy, just like yours. I had to do most o' the huntin' to keep us fed, and we never went hungry!" she laughed. "But I traded that'n off at the general store 'fore we left. Got me a pistol too!" she patted her belt as she spoke. She laughed again, "The storekeeper gave me a good deal cuz' when he got it, they called it a 'Storekeeper Special' cuz' o' it's short barrel. He din't like it, so..." she shrugged, grinning. "But I could use some practice with it, just a little. I ain't shot it yet an' I'd like to get used to it." She glanced to the trail and back to Cord, "Why, you thinkin' you might need a deputy to back you up with them Vaqueros?"

Cord grinned, "No, just wonderin' if you could take care of yourself if need be."

"Oh, I can do that alright. Might even help to take care of you, you know, like I done in the tavern with the chair!" she giggled, remembering when she cracked the chair over the head of the outlaw that was fighting Cord.

Cord laughed, "I knew you were dangerous with the furniture, but..." and shrugged.

26

QUESTIONS

THE VAQUERO SLID HIS HORSE TO A STOP AND SWUNG DOWN before the animal was settled. He hollered to the others, “Miguel! Miguel!” and ran to the side of the other vaqueros that were settled around the cookfire. The small herd of horses, numbering about twenty, were in the trees further up the draw and had been fenced in when the men weaved branches of the aspen among the alders and willows across the draw. They were camped just below the confluence of Willow Creek and the Rio Grande. The men, tired from the day’s drive and more, were gathered around the fire anticipating the meal of fresh venison and more.

Miguel Hernandez, the leader of the group, stood as he watched Esteban Morales draw near. Miguel frowned, motioned for Esteban to settle down and as he neared, Miguel, speaking in Spanish, responded,

"Now, what's all this about?" motioning the man to a seat on the end of the log nearby.

Esteban seated himself and looked at Miguel with a frown, "Do you remember the marshal we met when we first came with the herd? The one that visited with Señor Dawson afterwards?"

"Si, I remember," answered a frowning Miguel, seating himself on another log they had pulled near the fire. He looked at Esteban and waited for his explanation.

"I was talking to some miners, they agreed they needed horses, and as I left, I looked back and saw two riders come into the miner's camp. The one man rode a big grulla and was leading a pack mule, you remember that is what the marshal was riding. I went into the trees and looked back to be sure, and it was the marshal!"

"You said there were two riders, what about the other one?"

"I do not know. He was a smaller man on an Appaloosa and with a packhorse. But Miguel, if the marshal sees us with the horses, he will ask questions. Should we not leave?"

"No, we will not leave. If he gets too nosy—we will kill him! There are four of us, and only two of them. They know nothing, so..." he shrugged and reached for a willow that held a strip of venison over the fire.

"But Miguel, we do not have all the horses sold, and we do not have the money. These people, these

Americans, they hang horse thieves! And if the marshal catches us, we will hang!"

"¡Estás loco! One man cannot take us!" retorted Miguel, shaking his head as he pulled the meat from the stick.

"But...but...there are dos!"

Miguel chewed on his meat, looking around at the other men and nodded, "If we meet them, Jorgé and I will take the marshal. You and Elivé will take the other one. Easy, right?"

"Sí, Miguel, Sí."

Miguel looked around the circle to the other men, all of whom nodded their agreement, and then said, "Then let us get some sleep. We will start out early in the morning and get the horses sold and soon be on the trail back to Santa Fe!"

When Cord and Ema came from the box canyon of the Rio Grande, the trail kept to the high side of the river and where it turned east to go down valley. As the river pushed against the jutting shoulders of the mountains, the trail would take to the trees and often climb the shoulders until the river pushed back into the valley bottom. And when the meandering Rio Grande bent around Hogback Mountain to turn back to the north, the trail crossed Trout Creek, and true to its name, the creek gave up some nice trout to

Cord's hand-fishing technique and they were anticipating some fresh trout for supper.

As the river continued on its northward trek, it pushed itself against the shoulder of La Garita Caldera and crowded Cord and Ema into the aspen for their night's camp. Unknown to them at the time, the camp of the vaqueros was on the far side of the river and less than seven miles further downstream where the river bent back to the southwest.

As they sat by the fire after enjoying the meal of fresh trout and more, they both held cups of coffee in their hands and Cord had a Bible in his lap, unopened, and listened as Ema softly sang an old hymn,

Pass me not, O gentle Savior, Hear my humble cry;
While on others thou are smiling, Do not pass me by.
Savior, Savior, Hear my humble cry,
While on others thou art calling, Do not pass me by.
Let me at a throne of mercy, Find a sweet relief
Kneeling there in deep contrition, Help my unbelief.

She paused, a serious look on her face, and turned to Cord. "That's really about me, isn't it? I mean the words of the song. I did not know about Heaven before, and that song is asking for Jesus to *not pass me by.* And He didn't! You told me about Him and He heard my prayer and now..." She smiled, happy for her decision to accept the gift of eternal life as Cord had shown her.

She looked at Cord, glanced at the Bible, and asked, "Can I read that? Is it too hard?"

"It's not hard at all. You see, Em, this," he held up the Bible before him, "is God's love letter to his kids. And until you become one of His, it is hard to understand. But when you accept Christ and become a child of God, then it's easy to understand—just like a love letter from a father to his child."

"Can I read it?" she asked, holding out her hand for the Bible.

Cord grinned, "Sure," then opened the Bible to the first page of the gospel of John, "Start here, it says a lot and will help you on your day-by-day walk with Him."

Em accepted the Bible, looked at Cord and down at the opened pages and began to read to herself. After a moment, she looked up and smiled broadly, "Thanks!" and continued with her reading.

As darkness dropped its cloak on the land and the embers of the fire faded, Em was forced to give up on her reading and handed the Bible back to Cord, and quickly snuggled down into her blankets. Cord grinned, stood and did a little walkabout the camp, checking on the animals and with Blue by his side, he stepped to the edge of the trees and looked over the moonlit valley and up at the almost full moon overhead and said a quiet prayer of thanksgiving before turning around and going to his blankets.

As he lay in his blankets, his hands behind his head and the full moon high above, his thoughts were many. He glanced over at the still form of Emaline, smiled and wondered about her future, thought of his dream of a ranch and the ranch of John Dawson, looked at Em again and thought about a possible future together with her at his side. He grinned, thinking it was a pleasant thought, and rolled over and surrendered the night watch duties to Blue, who lay by his side, and Kwitcher who stomped at the aspen leaves and settled in for the night.

As they sat by the cookfire waiting on the coffeepot to start dancing and the sun to bring a little color to the day, Cord was deep in thought and was more quiet than Emaline was used to, causing her to glance his way often, frowning from her own thoughts. Finally he looked up at her and began, "The way I see it, if they're trying to sell stolen horses, they're gonna be mighty jumpy if I come around. They'll remember me from before and they'll know I'm a marshal..." he paused, letting his mind travel down the road of what-ifs before he looked up again, "and I don't want to put you in danger of any kind of shooting and such."

Em interrupted, "Now hold on there just a gol'-durned minit! I been takin' care of myself for some time now, even when I had my brother and father around, it was more like me takin' care o' them, not the other way around. So, don't you go thinkin' you gotta take care of me!" She growled as she banged the frying pan around, flipping the bacon and venison strips as she grumbled and frowned at Cord. "If anything, I'll hafta take care of you like I did back to the Forks with that big'un and the chair!" she grinned at the memory of using the armchair to keep Cord from getting choked by the one called Bull. She continued, "Mebbe you just oughta consider me a deputy or sumpin' like that. I got my pistol right here," as she patted the butt of the pistol showing above her belt at her belly, "an' I got muh rifle in the scabbard, so, I'm ready for anything!" She nodded and tucked her chin to emphasize her words.

Cord shook his head but had already learned about the strong-willed woman before him and he also knew she would probably best him in any argument, not because of smarts or logic but will. Cord chuckled as he was reminded of both his mother and sister and how they were much the same way. His father often said, *"Son, when a woman makes up her mind, you won't change it. All you can do is ride the storm and learn from it, and if you're lucky, you both will survive that storm and be better for it!"* Cord looked at Em and grinned, then held out his cup for some coffee, choosing to bite his tongue rather than risk an argument he would not win.

THE LONG AND wide valley of the Rio Grande stretched from east to west and the rising sun slowly climbed over the lower mountains, foothills of the San Juan mountain range, in the distance. The sky began to dance with the brilliant hues of pink and orange, the blazing lances shooting high into the few overhanging clouds, and the colors painted the valley of the Rio Grande in pale hues of the same colors. Muted shadows stretched away from the tall spruce that had shed the previous snowfall and now stood proudly with green branches swaying in the morning breeze.

It was a pleasant morning, but the disgruntled tones of the runaway vaqueros bit at one another. Arguments over coffee, liquor, and horses brought the anger of betrayal to the surface and Miguel shouted, "Aiieee, *callarse la boca*! Shut up! We have work to do! We must get these horses sold and delivered before anyone comes after us! We must get the money so we can go back to Santa Fe! We cannot do that with you arguing about everything! The next one that argues—*te dispararé!* I will shoot!"

The grumbling and staring with angry looks continued, but they were quiet about it until Elivé spoke up. "We must deliver eight of these horses to those in Willow. One man wants two teams of four and he has the gold to pay $200 per horse!"

"Good! Are any others sold? We have twenty left, and after those, that leaves twelve. We must sell them today—I want to be on the trail south by noon," declared Miguel.

"There are two camps with two each—past the confluence with Willow Creek. But there are other diggings with men I have not talked to yet," explained Elivé.

"After we go to Willow, you will go ahead up the valley to the other camps and get the rest of the horses sold. It will be easy for us," said Miguel, motioning to himself and the other two men, "to bring the rest. But you will need to point out the two camps for the other four horses."

"Sí," answered Elivé as he turned to fetch his mount as the others had done.

As the men gathered near, Miguel cautioned, "Remember, I will be in the lead. If we run into the marshal, I will talk to him and if he tries anything, I will take care of him. You," motioning to the rest of the men, "always watch and especially if the other one tries anything, kill him! We cannot have anyone knowing and coming after us!"

The three nodded, glanced to one another, and at Miguel's signal, went to the herd to break down the woven branches that served as a fence so they could start the drive to Willow.

27

SKIRMISH

THE SUN WAS JUST BEGINNING TO SHOW ITS FACE OVER THE eastern mountains at their back as Cord and Em watched their long shadows stretch before them. Cord had decided to ride straight to the mouth of Willow Creek gulch, which meant they had to cross the river where it bent back to the south. The Rio Grande had been their constant companion for the last couple days and had grown with the runoff of the recent snows, but it still was little more than a good-sized and still somewhat shallow creek. Where they chose to cross was just south of the bend at the double island that divided the waters. With shallows on both sides and the wider of the crossings being less than a hundred feet, it was an easy and quick crossing, never deep enough to touch the horses' bellies.

When they came through the water and busted through the cluster of willows, a low shoulder of old riverbank shielded them from view and Cord reined up, stepped down, and went to the crest for a look. Scanning the area with his binoculars, he spotted movement and a little bit of dust directly west, and it was more than just a couple riders. He nodded to himself, believing it was the vaqueros from the Dawson ranch with the horse herd.

As he turned to come to his feet, he was startled when Em asked, "What do you see?" She was standing directly behind him and shading her eyes as she looked in the distance. "Is that movement yonder the horses?"

Cord shook his head, took a deep breath as he stood, slipping the binoculars back into the case and answered, "I think so. I want to go there, maybe stop 'em and ask for their papers. If they're selling horses for Dawson, they should have something from him giving them the right to sell them. Now..." he paused as he motioned to the horses for them to mount up, "...it's not required because that's usually done on a handshake, but they probably don't know that. So, if they get spooked, we'll know they're in the wrong."

As they swung aboard, Cord looked back at Em and cautioned, "I know what you said about helpin', but I'd feel better if you'd try to stay out of it. If they start shooting, they probably won't care who they shoot at!"

"So, they won't know right off if I'm a girl, and they won't know that I'm armed and ready, so..." she grinned and shrugged.

Cord dropped his eyes and shook his head, "Have you *ever* done what you're told? About anything?" he asked.

"Once. But don't ask me when that was. Pa always talked about that one time, but I don't remember it," she giggled. "After that he quit tellin' me what to do and in his words, he just made suggestions!" She giggled again, enjoying Cord's obvious exasperation.

He looked at her, grinned, and thought to himself, *She is a firecracker but she's also durned good lookin' and there's that somethin' about her...but she makes me happy!* He glanced back at her and took in the view of the morning sun behind them and her reddish-blonde hair hanging from under her hat and catching the morning sunlight, and her womanly figure showing even with the linsey-Woolsey shirt and buckskin jacket that now hung open in the warmth of the morning. He took a deep breath and reminded himself to quit getting distracted from the possible problem before him with the horse herd.

They climbed the slight shoulder, took to the flats that had many seldom-used trails, probably mostly by deer and elk coming to water, and pointed their mounts to the mouth of Willow Gulch. This was where the trail of the horse herd and their trail would probably converge, but for now they were divided by Willow Creek.

Cord and Em came to the edge of the creek well ahead of the horse herd and Cord said, "We'll cross over, but that will be a giveaway to them that we are coming to them. So, be careful and stay well separate from me."

Em did not respond, just nodded and nudged her mount into the shallow creek to follow close behind Cord, Kwitcher, Blue and the pack mule. She also trailed a packhorse, but they were soon across the shallows and through the willows. The mouth of the gulch was one wide creek bottom, made so by many spring thaws and deep snows that overflowed the banks of the normally shallow creek. The flats on either side showed the signs of previous flooding with scattered scraps of driftwood, brush piles, clumps of brush that still held debris, and more. But on the far side, the horse herd that Cord estimated at about twenty to twenty-five horses and four riders, did not slow their drive.

Cord nudged Kwitcher to a trot to get to the trail ahead of the herd, reined up with Blue beside Kwitcher, and held up his hand for them to stop the herd. One rider was out front and quickly came to where Cord sat Kwitcher, as the others slowed the herd, getting them to stop by turning them back toward the flanks of the hills. Cord saw Blue's stance beside Kwitcher and knew the dog saw something he did not like. It was not often that the dog showed himself to be aggressive or overly protective, but there are times animals are better judges of character than men. Cord dropped his hand and casually leaned on his pommel, arms crossed with his right hand by his pistol and hidden behind his left arm. He grinned and nodded to the vaquero in the lead, recognized him as the one he met before and asked, "Miguel, isn't it?"

"Sí señor, and you are the marshal, correct?" he asked.

Cord glanced to the dog and spoke softly, "Easy boy, easy," then nodded to Miguel and said, "You've got quite a herd of horses here. They come from the Dawson ranch, I presume?"

"Sí, sí. We are delivering them to some of the miners."

"Good, then you won't mind if I check your bill of sale, or bills, as it may be." Cord watched the expression on Miguel's face change from friendly to angry and added, "I'm sure Mr. Dawson gave you the papers for the miners, did he not?" asked Cord, still forcing a smile as he casually grasped the grip on his pistol. He did not know exactly where Em was but he felt her near and could not take his eyes off Miguel. Cord also saw another of the vaqueros coming closer, off to his right a little, apparently trying to get on both sides of him, but he heard movement slightly behind him as a horse kicked a stone. He saw both Miguel and the other vaquero stop, look past him, and smile as Miguel spoke, "Senorita! I am surprised!"

Miguel looked at Cord and, nodding toward Em, asked, "Is this your woman?" What Cord did not see was Em had stopped, removed her hat and shook her hair loose and the morning sunlight seemed to illuminate the golden red of her hair and she smiled broadly, catching the full attention of the vaqueros.

Before he answered Miguel, Cord heard Em say, "No, we're just riding together," in a bit of a flippant tone and Cord forced himself to keep from smiling. But her presence had stopped the second man who relaxed and leaned on the big saddle-horn of his hand-tooled saddle. His thoughts had suddenly turned from anticipating a shooting to wondering about the woman. It was one thing to shoot a man, even a lawman, but to shoot a woman in this land where women were more scarce than big nuggets, it was something no one would tolerate.

Cord asked again, "The papers?" and watched as Miguel feigned reaching into his coat with his left hand, but Cord saw him grabbing at his pistol with his right. Blue launched himself at the vaquero as Cord brought his pistol to bear just an instant before Miguel and both guns stabbed fire, startling the horses and their mounts. Blue also struck with fangs bared, eyes blazing and his full weight behind him. Cord had never seen the dog jump so high, and Blue sunk his teeth into the gun arm of Miguel just as he started to pull the trigger again.

With the attack of the dog, the blasts of gunfire, the suddenness of the attack, the horse of Miguel jerked to the side, dropped his head between his front hooves and did his best with his hind feet to rearrange the few clouds in the blue sky. The wounded Miguel valiantly tried to keep his seat, but Cord saw the red blossom of blood on the man's chest and with the bullet wound, the attack of the dog who had not released his bite and still hung his entire weight on the man's arm, the vaquero planted his face in the dust as his mount bucked away from the commotion.

Cord grabbed at his side, knowing he had been hit, but he could not give in to the pain. Kwitcher was accustomed to Cord's movements and even the sudden blasts of gunshots. Cord had trained the horse to stay solid when he shot from the saddle, as he occasionally did when hunting meat. Cord glanced toward the other man just in time to see him also trying for his pistol but before Cord could bring his to bear, the blast from behind him sent a lance of fire and smoke to carry the lead bullet into the man's shoulder, followed immediately by another bullet that blossomed on his chest and drove him back, unseating him as well.

The horse herd started to bolt and the other two vaqueros whose first thoughts were always about the herd, quickly rallied after the animals, neither one joining the shooting, but going after the horses. Cord looked back at Em and saw a wide-eyed, open-mouthed, pale girl tightly gripping her short-barreled pistol that still had a thin wisp of smoke curling from the barrel. She did not move until her face started to melt into a mask of fear and sadness as she realized she had just shot a man who lay in the dust, face down, and was unmoving and probably dead.

Cord stepped down, pistol still in hand, and walked cautiously to the side of Miguel, who had struggled to sit up, but fell back on his side and looked up at Cord, "We were going. . . back...home..." and frowning, Miguel started to lift his empty hand to Cord then breathed his last. Cord looked over at the second man who lay face down and unmoving, then walked back to Em who still sat in her saddle, the pistol in her hand, but resting on the pommel.

Cord gently took the pistol and said, "You might want to get down and take a seat over there," nodding to some rocks by a couple of skinny cottonwoods. He helped her down, handed her the rifle and often looking at the herding activity of the other two vaqueros, he stayed wary as he helped Em to a seat. She put her pistol away, lay the rifle across her knees and taking a heavy sigh, she turned to watch the rest of the round-up of strays.

Cord was watchful as the men circled the herd, let them settle down and then he started to step back aboard Kwitcher, but felt a stabbing pain in his side and stumbled slightly, pulled his arm away from his side and saw his hand covered in blood. He chose to walk toward the nearest man, keeping his pistol in his right hand hanging at his side, his left arm holding his jacket tight to his side. As he neared, he called out, "Keep your hands where I can see them!"

The man answered, "Sí señor, we expected you,

and Miguel told us we would have to kill you and the other one, but we did not know she was a woman! And we, me an' Jorgé, did not want to kill anyone," he added, motioning to his partner and himself.

"So, the horses are stolen?"

"Sí señor, but Jorgé and me, we did not know they were stolen at first. Miguel just told us to go with him, we did not know he would steal them. Miguel just told us the horses would be payment for our work and we would drive them to the miners and get the money we needed to return to our families. We just wanted to go home to Santa Fe."

"And your name?" asked Cord.

"I am Esteban, Esteban Morales." With a nod to his partner, he explained, "He is Jorgé Medino. We came north with Señor Dawson. We were going to try for gold, but we know nothing about the getting of gold. So..." he shrugged and he motioned to the horses.

"I tell you what Esteban. If you and Jorgé help me get these two buried, and help me take the horses back to Señor Dawson, I'll put in a good word for you and maybe..." he shrugged, putting one hand to the side, palm up, and suggesting the possibility of no charges.

"Sí, sí, we can do that," he answered, nodding to Jorgé and back to Cord. "Do we go back today?"

"Prob'ly," replied Cord. "Just move 'em o'er there by the grass and the water. That'll keep 'em happy till we're ready. You and Jorgé get down and come with me to the packs, we'll get some shovels to start the buryin'."

As they neared the stack of gear, Cord motioned them to the packs, walked to Em and spoke softly, "I took a bullet," and she jumped to her feet before he said another word. He held up his hand and said, "Now hold on—they need to get the buryin' done, and while they're doin' that, we'll take their weapons and let 'em work. Then you can take care of this," he said, pointing to his side. "Just act like ever'thing's alright. You can do it!"

28

TRAIL DRIVE

WHILE THE TWO VAQUEROS SET ABOUT DIGGING THE graves for their compadres, Cord surrendered to the attentions of Ema. The wound from the bullet of Miguel was a furrow of open flesh and blood that cut across the top of his hip bone. It was painful and Cord had lost a lot of blood. Ema had him stretched out on a blanket and had started a small fire to warm some water and more. Cord watched as she had a forked branch of a willow that held a pad of prickly pear cactus over the small flames and when she noticed his expression as he watched, "They're good for your wound. I'll peel the casing off, use the soft pulp directly on the wound and bandage it up. That'll stop the bleeding, help the pain, and cleanse the wound."

Cord frowned, "Where'd you learn that?"

"Ah, Pa told us about it when we was comin' out

on the wagon train. Dunno who showed him, but we used it before—works good too. When I get that wound cleaned, I'm also gonna use some Balm of Gilead, it's made from aspen buds and it helps too. But now that you're payin' attention, drink some o' that tea there. Made it from the willow bark—it'll help the pain."

"Well, don't you beat all. Good cook, good nurse, and good lookin'. But you sure are bossy!" he chuckled as he reached for the cup of willow tea. He looked over at the two vaqueros busy at the digging and quietly asked Em, "They give you any trouble?"

"Nope. Got their rifles and pistols layin' right there," he said, nodding to the stack of weapons beside the log nearby. "But I'm thinkin' they're gonna be plum peaceable."

"Hope so...it'll take us a couple days to get back to La Loma and the Dawson Ranch, and we need them to get it done. I was wonderin' why some of Dawson's other riders haven't come lookin' for the horses."

"Maybe they'll show up soon, but if not," began Em, taking the pads from the fire and laying them on a nearby rock, "we'll need to get started soon anyway. I don't relish the idea of havin' to tend to you *and* them too!"

"You just bandage me up. I can still ride and ramrod them," declared Cord. He stretched out a hand to rub Blue behind the ears. The dog had stayed by his side from the time of the attack, he had sensed something then and was still concerned about his master now and would not leave his side. Cord gave a lopsided grin as he talked to Blue then looked back at a grinning Em and asked, "Whaaatt?"

"Men and their dogs," she declared with a slight smile and a shake of her head.

"Hey, I've known plenty women that were just like men when it comes to their dogs. And I've also noticed Blue here makin' up to you and you've been payin' a lot of attention to him. I was beginning to wonder if he forgot all about me!"

"You blame him?" giggled Em.

Cord just shook his head and braced himself for her ministrations to his wound.

THE SUN WAS at its zenith when Cord and the vaqueros started the small herd of horses on the trail back to the Dawson Ranch. It was familiar country for Cord as he took the point and led the wranglers and the horses across the Rio Grande and start south on the trail that sided the river. The animals were well rested, fed and watered and moved easily on the trail. There was always that homing sense within the equine that told them they were headed back home and they moved readily, heads high and tails flagging. They had traveled about five miles when they came to the head of the canyon that some were already calling the Rio Grande Palisades. Cord led the herd to cross the river again to take to the trail that sided the river on the broad shoulder of the west side.

They rode in the shadows of the high pillars of volcanic rock that stood tall above them, stretching 1200 to 1500 feet taller than the valley bottom, standing shoulder to shoulder like a garrison of stone soldiers guarding the dark canyon below. The three levels of stone columns appeared to be the very pillars that held the blue of heaven high above. The clatter of hooves, the occasional grunts, blows, snorts and squeals of the horses bounced off the steep rock walls of the canyons and came back upon them to stifle even the crashing and splashing of the white water rapids.

The sudden opening of the canyon walls marked the sloping shoulder that held the burgeoning village of Wagon Wheel Gap but Cord did not slow the herd as they drove the animals right down the middle of the only street of the popular supply stop for the influx of prospectors. Cord saw the storekeeper, Toots Monroe, standing on his boardwalk in his ever-present apron, and waving at Cord as he rode past. Just the presence of the man brought back many memories of his earlier days in the little settlement, but Cord just grinned, returned the wave and kept moving. High above the village, more palisades stood tall, marking the flat top of the broad mesa above the town, and pushed the walls of the canyon closer forcing the herd to keep to the shelf road that cut across the talus slope that fell from high above. Once again, the clatter of hooves echoed back from the canyon walls and the town fell behind them.

When the river made a wide bend around a point of land that pushed away from the high mesa and moved the river around that bend, it afforded a good slope with tall timber above and a grassy flat beside the water that would give a good place to hold the horses and make camp. Cord reined up, herded the animals closer to the water which allowed them to stop and roll, grab a mouthful of grass and stop their progress. Cord signaled the two vaqueros to make the stop and by stretching out a couple lengths of riata, intertwined with the brush and cottonwoods, they soon had a good corral for the animals.

As Em moved past the herd and joined Cord, she asked, "This where we're makin' camp for the night?"

"Umhmm," as he nodded to a grassy flat on a slight shoulder above the rope corral and overlooking the water. "We'll have a cook fire there, picket our horses in the cottonwoods, and should have an easy night of it."

"What about them?" asked Em, as she nodded toward the vaqueros that were finishing the riata corral.

"We'll eat together, take turns on guard. I think

they'll be alright, they seem to be eager to get back to the ranch, so...I reckon they aren't too concerned about Dawson's reaction. They said they didn't know Miguel had stolen the herd, they thought he was selling them for Dawson, but...I dunno. Hard to say for sure."

"Well, Pa always said it was best to err on the side of caution. Course he was talkin' 'bout hard rock minin', but it applies to men too!"

Cord chuckled, "All men?"

Em laughed, "Prob'ly! Now, go get me some firewood!"

UNKNOWN TO CORD, Em made a quick stop at the store in Wagon Wheel Gap and resupplied with bacon, flour, and coffee and a few other essentials, so she set about making a good batch of bacon, beans, and biscuits for their supper which was eagerly enjoyed by all. Esteban was the first to say, "Gracias, señorita. It has been a long time since we had a good meal cooked by a woman."

"Sí, señorita, it is ver' good!" added Jorgé, grinning broadly between bites of his biscuit.

Em answered, "Thank you, thank you very much," and looked sidelong at Cord, waiting to see if he added his praises as well.

Cord grinned, "Yes it is! Very good! Best beans, bacon, and biscuits I've had all day!" and chuckled as he took another bite, but had to quickly duck out of the way of the thrown biscuit that came from a scowling Emaline.

With a last check of the horses and the riata surround, Cord joined the others at the remains of the cookfire and sat as they finished the last of the coffee. Cord looked at Esteban, "So, you two want to take a turn at standing guard?" he asked, looking from one to the other.

"Si, we can do that," answered Esteban with a glance to his partner, who also nodded.

"Well, I'm going to trust the two of you. Like I told you earlier, you do a good job on this return to the Dawson ranch and I'll put in a good word for you to Mr. Dawson. I'm sure he'll be glad to have two good vaqueros back at work. He told me before that he was anxious to get back to Santa Fe, and he needs trustworthy vaqueros to take care of the animals he has on the ranch. He said once that he hoped Miguel would take over the running of the ranch, but since that's not going to happen, what do you think he'll do? Is there someone else that could run the place?"

The two men frowned, looked at one another and both shrugged as Esteban looked at Cord, "I do not know, señor. Several of the men went to the mountains to try for gold, a few came back, empty-handed. But...I don't know who he could have as a *gerente,* how you say, manager."

"Well, I'll take first watch and I'll wake you, Esteban, and you can take a couple hours and wake Jorgé for his turn," to which both men responded with a nod and a "Sí, señor."

While the two vaqueros rolled out their blankets and stretched out, Cord went to the cookfire where Em was also stretching out her blankets. He glanced at the woman as the firelight danced in her reddish-gold tresses and smiled, *she gets more beautiful every time I look at her,* he thought, then shook his head as he said, "I'll be makin' the rounds. You try to get some good sleep, if you can. I know you're a little skittish about those two, but I think they'll be alright."

"I hope so," she mumbled and smiled up at Cord as she crawled beneath her blankets.

She watched as he walked away from the glow of the fire and started toward the edge of the herd down by the river's edge. The chuckle of the river water was almost mesmerizing as Cord walked through the moonlit grass and watched the milling of the horses. Most had already found a spot of their own and stood hipshot, heads hanging and resting. A few had even stretched out in the cool grass and lay on their side.

While Jorgé and Estéban had turned their mounts in with the herd, Cord and Em had picketed their mounts and pack animals together and nearer the camp. Blue walked with Cord and they made their way around the entire camp, walking easily and quietly, enjoying the cool, moonlit night. Shadows danced in the trees as the gentle breezes of the night swayed the forest to its own music of the mountains and Cord hummed one of his favorite hymns, *Nearer My God to Thee,* and he was thinking of the second verse, *Though like the wanderer, the sun gone down, darkness be over men, my rest a stone; yet in my dreams I'd be nearer, my God to thee.*

But the low rumble of a growl from Blue stopped him cold. He dropped the rifle from his shoulder to his grip before him as he lowered to a bit of a crouch and began to look where Blue was looking. The growl of Blue rumbled deep in his chest, but the dog was frozen in place as he stared at the edge of the trees that marched down the steep black slope of the mountain behind him. Cord could see nothing moving, glanced down to Blue and back to the trees, when suddenly an ear-piercing scream split the darkness with the predator's screech of the night hunter catamount. The cougar or mountain lion, the fearful hunter with talons and fangs and night-piercing vision. It was the scream became a series of coughs and spits, then all sound was swallowed by the dark blanket of night. The startled and nervous horses had whinnied and screamed, pushing and shoving one another, but now paced nervously. Cord ran to the brush of the riata corral, saw the two vaqueros already at the edge of the herd, hands extended and speaking softly to the horses, trying to calm them.

Cord went to the packs and grabbed the rifles of the vaqueros and carried them to the two men, "Be ready! I don't think he'll jump 'em, but...be ready! I'm going to make a round again, maybe see him before he attacks!"

Cord walked off into the night, Blue at his side, looking for the catamount of the cliffs.

29

CHAOS

Silence reigned as Cord moved with Blue, slowly and soundless, working the edge of the trees and the stretch of grass between the pines and the river. Nothing moved nor made a sound. The usual noises of the night, the hooting of hunting owls, the screech of searching eagles and hawks, the soft melodies of meadowlarks, or the distant lonesome calls of the coyotes, had all surrendered the coliseum of the canyon to the catamount and silence lay like a downy blanket along the skirts of the slopes. Nothing stirred. Even the horses had settled with the presence of the vaqueros who hummed a soft serenade to quiet their spirits and put their minds on peaceful things.

Cord, without realizing what he was doing, took only shallow breaths, and those between steps, careful not to let even a whisper hinder his hearing. Blue moved on softly padded paws, choosing each step carefully. Each step of the companion hunters was preceded by searching, watching for movement, listening for even the sound of ragged breathing, but nothing came. Cord made a careful and complete circuit of the camp but found nothing. He came alongside Esteban and spoke in a whisper, "I think he has moved on, but we'll all need to be watchful for a while longer. We'll build up the fire, maybe that will discourage him. I will wait a bit, then make another round."

Esteban nodded, whispered, "Did you see him?"

"No, just heard him. He was up there in the black timber and I think he moved across the face of the hill there below that first line of cliffs. He was too close for comfort and probably thought we were too close to him."

Esteban nodded, held his rifle close to his chest and searched the darkness and listened for any movement. He watched as Cord moved toward the remains of the campfire where Emaline waited, standing beside the glowing coals, rifle in hand as she too searched the tree line. As Cord neared, he spoke softly, "We're coming in, Em, don't shoot!"

Em relaxed, giggled a little and said, "I think I can tell the difference between you and a cougar. The cougar has a longer tail!" and muffled another giggle as she watched Cord come close. He lay the rifle on the log, started moving about gathering up more firewood and explained, "I'm gonna build up the fire—maybe that will keep him at bay."

"Suits me! Ain't gonna get any sleep anyway! Might as well put some more coffee on too."

The rest of the night, although everyone was restless, was for the most part peaceful. The horses were still a bit skittish, but none tried the barriers and with first light, the animals settled down and the breakfast prepared by Em was enjoyed by the men. Cord made a circuit of the camp with Blue at his side, and the dog was not alarmed and apparently did not pick up the scent of a cougar nearby.

When he returned to the camp, Cord said, "Let's pack it up and get on the trail. I'd just as soon get as far from here as we can just as soon as we can!"

The two vaqueros met that remark with smiling faces and nodding heads and many remarks that included the oft-used words, "Sí señor!" The riatas were quickly gathered and coiled and the horses started on the trail showing they were just as anxious as the herders as they moved with a quick pace that put the night's campsite well behind them.

The canyon seemed to spread its arms wide and welcomed the morning's warmth and brightness. The slopes of the palisades tapered to the edges of the flat-topped mesas that sided the canyon, giving an easier slope for the thicker timber. As Cord lifted his eyes to the mountainsides, he also realized the thick timber afforded better cover for a hunting predator and Cord stood in his stirrups to try to see down canyon, fearful of any place where the trail might afford a promontory for an attack by a hungry cat. He glanced at Blue who seemed to be watchful but staying near and Kwitcher's ears were fidgety, flicking back and forth and the big stallion was tensing up and high stepping. Cord slipped the rifle from the scabbard and lay it across his pommel and as he crested a slight rise in the trail, he reined up and searched the surroundings.

Thick black timber stood heavy on the shoulder of the slope on the west edge, well above Cord's left shoulder. Scattered ponderosa, cottonwoods, and willows grew close on the banks of the river to his right. He knew if any attack came from the cat, it would be from the timber. He looked about, knowing the predator preferred a high rocky escarpment that would overlook the trail and afford cover, and just such a spot was no more than twenty yards ahead.

Cord nudged Kwitcher with knee pressure to step forward and the big stallion moved tentatively, each step cautiously taken, but still responsive to his rider. They dropped over the slight rise and Cord watched the rocky prominence, looking for movement but there was nothing. A ruckus behind him followed by shouts and screaming whinnies brought Cord around and digging heels to Kwitcher. He immediately knew the cougar had attacked the herd behind him, probably on the narrow portion that was the closest to the timber.

He jacked a round into the chamber of the Winchester and stretched low on the neck of the big horse. They crested the rise with Blue at their side and Kwitcher jerked to the side, narrowly missing a collision with several of the stampeded horses. Cord kept his seat, searching for the puma and saw the dust and ruckus less than twenty yards ahead. Kwitcher fidgeted, fought the reins, but Cord forced his will with a strong hand and deep stirrups with heels in his ribs.

In an instant, Cord saw the tawny coat of the cougar, blood at his mouth, fangs showing as he glared at the intruder and growled as he kept his claws deep in the meat of the neck of the grey mare beneath him. Cord fired once and again, the blasts of the rifle racketing down the canyon, and the cougar flinched, but tensed, ready to launch himself at both Cord and Kwitcher. Another rifle sounded, and another, and Cord fired again. The rattle of rifle fire sounded like a war had broken out in the canyon, echoes multiplying the blasts and bouncing again and again on the palisades of the canyon.

Cord saw the beast flinch again and again and suddenly fall still. The grey horse that had been the prey also lay still, eyes glazed and unmoving. Cord was breathing heavily as he swung to the ground and slowly approached the bloody scene, shaking his head but stepping carefully. As he neared the beast, he reached out with the muzzle of his rifle and jabbed the ribs of the cougar and there was no response. Cord stepped back, breathed deep and looked up to see Emaline and Esteban standing near one another, both with rifles before them and both rifles with a thin whisper of smoke rising from the muzzles.

"He's dead. Esteban, go help Jorge round up the horses. I'll get this off the trail," he said, nodding to the carcasses of the horse and cougar, "and come help. This will have to be buried or something, otherwise won't nothing come past here." He knew most of the horses and Jorge had turned back on the trail to escape the attack and would have to come this way to get to the ranch. With a nod to Em, Cord went to the mule that was trailing behind the packhorse of Em and retrieved a shovel to begin the task of burying the carcass.

After Cord buried the carcass of the cougar, he dragged the carcass of the horse into the trees and covered it with dirt and more. Esteban and Jorge were busy rounding up the spooked horses and it was midday before they brought the remains of the herd back down the trail, although there were still a few that had fled down the trail past Cord when the attack occurred. Em had busied herself making coffee and biscuits to go with the strip steaks that hung over the cookfire and the meal was greatly appreciated by all.

Another hour or so on the trail and they came from the canyon and made a short stop at the fork in the river. It had already been a long day and a trying one and Cord condescended to make camp for the night and go the rest of the way tomorrow. At the mouth of the canyon, a Barlow and Sanderson Stage stop welcomed the herders and offered to have the men join them for the evening meal that was already on the cookstove in anticipation of the coming stage. With minimal effort, Cord and the vaqueros made a camp by the river and another riata corral for the tired horses that had traveled the trail more than once in their flight and round-up.

Em especially enjoyed the idea of having a meal inside the stage stop and a meal that had been prepared by another woman. The two women spent much of the afternoon visiting as they both worked at preparing the meal, female companionship was a rarity and to be enjoyed.

30

CHANGES

"So, honey. How long you been travelin' with that marshal?" asked Lottie. She was the wife of the station keeper for the Barlow and Sanderson stage line and the only wife found in any of the existing stage stops for the company. She and her husband, Zedekiah Wooten, had started a farm in the area called South Fork where the south fork of the Rio Grande merged with the big river. When the stage company set up their line, the Wooten couple volunteered their cabin for a station and they were already enjoying the company of the travelers even though there had only been a couple stages pass through. The older woman, older by no more than five or six years, smiled at Emaline as she asked the question and waited with hands in the biscuit dough for the answer.

Emaline smiled, "Oh, just a few days. He knew muh pa and me'n muh pa and my brother had a mining claim up to the forks of the Animas and, well, after the outlaws kilt muh pa, we," nodding toward the marshal who was seated just outside the front door on the porch with Lottie's man, "met up at the saloon. He was fightin' with the outlaws and I he'ped him a mite. So, we was headin' for Saguache to catch the stage there. Din't know the stage had come this far!"

"Goin' far?" asked Lottie.

"Don' rightly know," drawled Em, dropping her eyes and speaking softly. "Got some relatives back east, I think, and this is the first time I've ever been alone, so it seemed like the only thing to do was to go back there. Don' really wanna go back, don' hardly know 'em." She looked at the bowl of potatoes she had started peeling and reached for another.

"You think you'd rather stay with him, don't cha?" asked Lottie, nodding in the direction of the front porch where Cord sat talking with Lottie's husband, Zedekiah.

Em let a slow smile paint her face as she glanced to the porch, then nodded to Lottie. "Reckon. He's the only friend I got, but...he's more'n that. But I've only known him a few days! My momma used to say love is like a flower, it takes time to grow! But..." she dropped her eyes and fell quiet and contemplative.

"Well, I've seen some flowers that take a long time to blossom, others that spring up overnight and bloom just as purty as you please. Now it sounds all well an' good to talk about love in purty colors, smells, and such, but that's not real love. It's more'n a feelin'. You know that giddy feelin' you get when you look at the one you're thinkin' about, the one that makes your stomach do flip flops and such. Oh, that might feel alright for a while, but those feelin's can change. You know, like the weather. One day all sunny and bright, the next all dark an' stormy. No, no, no. That's not real love, uh-uh." She paused as she worked the dough, punched it down, and splattered some loose flour about.

She chuckled, pushed a loose bunch of hair back above her ear with a flour-coated hand, then put knuckles on her hips and turned to face Em. "You see, honey, love is somethin' special and God tells us about it in simple terms, so all of us can understand it. He says in John 3:16 *For God so loved the world that he gave his only begotten Son, that whosoever believeth in him should not perish, but have everlasting life.* Now listen to that part again, *so loved that he gave...* See, love is self-sacrifice. He loved—He gave. And because of that, it's something that grows, always grows. He loved—He gave. And when we love, we don't take, we give, and give, and give. That's what love is—self-sacrifice. We give of our time, our talents, our treasure, whatever we are and whatever we have. Because the one we love is deserving of all we are and have. And when we are loved in that same way, we receive too, but that's another lesson in another time." She chuckled as she returned to her dough, smiling broadly.

Em pondered what she heard for a moment, then with a simple smile said, “You’re right, Lottie. That’s what I saw ‘tween my ma and pa. Both of ‘em, givin’ to each other, all the time and always happy about it.” She paused, reflecting, and a little quieter added, “’bout killed Pa when we lost her. He couldn’t hardly do much, didn’t say much, he was a different man after that.”

Lottie thought it best to change the subject a mite and asked, “So, whereabouts back east are you goin’?”

Em dropped her eyes, shook her head slowly, “Not rightly sure, probably some place in Kentucky called Paducah. Got some family there, but...” she shrugged. Then with another thought, she lifted her face to Lottie, “Say, what stages come thru here an’ where they goin’?”

Lottie laughed and said, “Only had a couple so far. They come from Denver City and from Cañon City. They come through here goin’ to Lake City and thereabouts. Ain’t had none come back thisaway yet, so don’ know ‘bout them. I think Zed has him a notebook with what they wanna have for a schedule, but that’s subject to change after the driver gets used to the roads and such.”

“So, you don’t know ‘bout stages comin’ through here and goin’ back east?” asked Em.

“Not yet,” replied Lottie, knowing exactly what the girl was thinking. “Maybe you could just stay here a spell till they get it figgered out, help me do some cookin' and such, until you get things settled in your mind," she suggested, and adding *in your heart* in her silent thoughts with a smile. "Sides, I could always use the comp'ny!"

Em smiled and replied, "Well, I do kinda like that idea, seein' as how I ain't got nobody waitin' on me anywhere. I'll see what Cord has to say 'bout it. I don't know what he's got planned, he might just be thinkin' 'bout gettin' shut o' me by goin' to Saguache, but, well..." she shrugged.

"Oh honey, I've seen the way he looks at you and kinda hovers around you, he ain't thinkin' 'bout gettin' shut o' you, ummhmmm, no, he's got other things on *his* mind," Lottie chuckled, punching the dough before her.

"So, Cord, how ya' like bein' a marshal?" asked Zed, puffin' on his corn-cob pipe and rocking back in his rocking chair, looking sidelong at the younger man.

"Oh, well, I guess it's like my dad used to say, 'Everybody's gotta do their part when it comes to building a country. Some gotta do the plowin', some preachin', some peddlin', and some policin'.' Takes all of us, but I don't plan on doin' it much longer. I always had a hankerin' to have a farm or ranch, raise crops and cattle. I like the idea of puttin' sweat into the land instead of blood. If all the outlaws would just quit their outlawin' it'd be a lot simpler. But my preacher father said, 'Man is born to sin and it takes a godly nation to stand up for what is right.' That time might be coming, but not soon enough for me. I talked to a fella down south from here, the man that put in the ranch where these horses came from, John Dawson, and he was talking about getting the ranch all set up and havin' one of his men run it for him, while he goes back to Sante Fe and his new wife. Now, that's the kind of place I'd like to have some day, but what little I make on the marshal job, prob'ly won't allow that to happen."

"What about a family? Don't you want to have a family someday?" asked Zed, making his rocking chair protest his movement as he leaned back.

"I do. Oh, I was married before, served as both marshal and county sheriff up in Oro City, but my wife died in childbirth; both she and the baby passed." He paused, dropping his eyes to the floor of the porch, then with a heavy sigh and a deep breath, "So, maybe one day..." he drawled.

Zed grinned, nodded, "Ummhmm, I understand. She 'pears to be a right nice little filly! With a woman like that, you'd raise a crop of young'uns if nuthin' else!" he laughed, coughed, spat out some loose tobacco from the pipe and continued laughin' as he looked at Cord's red face.

———

As dusk lowered its curtain of darkness, the group gathered around the table and Zed led them in a prayer of thanksgiving for the bounty and the company and with his "Amen" the meal began. The stage had not yet come and Zed explained, "There is no real schedule, just a need to be prepared so if it shows, we can feed 'em and change the team and send them on the way. The driver said last time they was hopin' to get a schedule lined out, but they had make a few runs just to get a better idea of time and such. So..." he shrugged and passed the bowl of potatoes. The conversation continued through the meal and past, and everyone soon turned in for the night. Cord and the vaqueros spent the night in the barn while Em rolled out her blankets in front of the fireplace in the home.

Come morning, at the breakfast just about first light, Cord agreed that it would be best for Em to stay with the Wootens until he returned from delivering the horses. "I shouldn't be more'n a couple days, three at most. And maybe by then the stage drivers will give Zed a better idea of what routes and times the stages will be traveling. And then, if we have to, we can go on to Saguache and catch an eastbound stage," he explained, and added almost as a mumble, "if that's still what you want to do."

Em frowned, "What *I* want to do? That was more your idea than mine!" she stated with a question on her face.

"We'll talk about it when I get back. I just want to

get you settled somewhere safe until...” Cord shrugged, dropping his eyes and turning toward the door.

Em lifted her eyebrows and let a slow smile paint her face as she glanced to Lottie and back to Cord. She just shook her head slowly and looked again to Lottie, “Reckon I’ll get the table cleaned off and we can get started on a meal for the stage.”

31

DAWSON RANCH

THE HERD OF HORSES STRETCHED OUT WITH CORD RIDING point and the vaqueros alternating between flanker and drag, but the animals needed little tending. The homing instinct in the horses had already shown itself as the string stepped out into a ground-eating trot, heads high, manes flying in the wind and the quick pace kept Kwitcher on the move, but it was a pace the long-legged grulla stallion enjoyed and he too had his head held high and mane flying. Blue ran beside him and often looked over his shoulder at Cord who sat high in the saddle, occasionally having to grab his hat to keep it from flying in the wind.

The almost twenty miles from the stage station to the ranch was behind them before the sun reached its zenith in the azure, blue cloudless sky. As the herd neared the front gate of the ranch, Cord went ahead to open the gate wide and stood beside it, Kwitcher at his back, as they watched the herd move into the ranch grounds and head right to the large corral beside the barn. Jorgé was in the lead and bent down to open the gate, swung it wide for the animals to pass through. Once inside the corral, the horses milled about, many tossing their heads and crowding one another, all content to be home again.

Cord rode in and reined up, stepped down, and joined Jorgé and Estéban at the fence. Cord looked at the men, "So, you ready to fess up with Mr. Dawson, tell him what happened and what you want to do?"

"Sí señor, it is best we do that," said Estéban, glancing to Jorgé.

Cord saw movement on the porch of the hacienda and said, "Here he comes now, so…" he shrugged. Both men turned and stepped back nearer the fence, the apprehension showing on their faces.

"Well, hello!" declared John Dawson. The stern-looking man was dressed in his usual linen shirt, buckskin jacket, wool trousers, and boots, but was without his customary hat and his receding hairline showed the tufts of white hair blowing in the wind. His Van Dyke moustache and beard gave him the distinguished look of a southern gentleman, but his piercing eyes also told of suspicion and repressed anger. He stepped closer to Cord, extended his hand to shake and greeted, "Marshal, it's good to see you." He glanced into the corral and saw the milling horses and looked sternly at the two vaqueros and growled, "Where's Miguel and Elivé?"

Cord spoke up, "They're dead. And as you've

probably guessed, Miguel was the one that was responsible for your missing herd. We met up just south of Willow. I guessed something was amiss and I asked Miguel for the papers on the horses, but he thought he should try to answer that question with his pistol, but..." Cord shrugged, and continued, "Elivé also tried and joined his friend. They're buried there. But these two," Cord said, "were a different story. They agreed to help me bring your horses back and I said I'd put in a good word for them. Esteban said they did not know Miguel stole the horses, they were told to help drive them to deliver them to the miners. But on the way, they realized what had happened and when they could have jumped in the fight against me, they went after the horses instead. So, whatever happens now, is up to you, Mr. Dawson."

"How many did you bring back?" asked the rancher.

"Counting those ridden by the men, twenty."

"That means we lost ten." He looked at Esteban, "Where's the others?"

"Miguel had sold them and the miners have them, Sí, but the money he got, we have. The pouches of gold are in my saddlebags," explained a repentant Esteban.

"And you two want to stay on?" asked John.

"Sí señor," replied Esteban, glancing to Jorgé and back to Dawson.

"Good, good. Well, the cook's got a meal ready in

the dinner shack, so go eat and I'll be in to give you your orders for the day," ordered a stern-faced Dawson.

As the men led their horses to the barn to strip them of their gear, John turned to Cord and asked, "How 'bout you comin' in the house? I've got a few questions for you."

"Sure, I can do that, long as you got some good coffee!" declared Cord, tying Kwitcher to the rail fence and loosening the cinch to let him rest.

THE HOME, although still in need of a few finishing touches, was an impressive structure. Built in the hacienda style with adobe walls and big timber beams, polished stone floors and many windows, had a homey feel to it, provided by the two matronly women who busily buzzed about tending to every need of the *patrón.* One of the women greeted Cord at the door, took his hat and jacket and motioned him to a chair opposite Dawson in the main room.

"I'm impressed!" declared Cord as he seated himself, "I did not expect so grand a home in such a short time."

Dawson smiled, nodded, and explained, "I had a good crew of many craftsmen. I wanted the home to be finished before I brought my new wife up here, but..." he shrugged and frowned as he looked at Cord.

The expression on the man's face told Cord there was more to his remark than he let on but Cord chose to let it be until and if Dawson chose to explain.

The women brought the coffee and a plate of treats that Dawson described as, "The ones with sugar are called *conchas* and the others have an apple filling and they are called *empanadas*. Those are my favorites. Go ahead, help yourself!" he motioned as he leaned forward to pick one of the *empanadas*.

As the men enjoyed the treat, Dawson began, "I know last time we met, you talked about trying to finish things up so you could put the marshal job behind you. Do you think you've done that? I know it surprised me to see you bringing in the herd of horses, so I'm guessing you've been pretty busy."

Cord grinned as he dipped the *concha* in his coffee, took a tasty bite and nodded with a grin at Dawson, "Well, it has been a busy few weeks, that's for sure. We caught the gang that was jumpin' all the claims and killin' the miners. Shot two in the confrontation in a bar, held the others for trial and they were hanged. I think with the coming of winter, most of the outlaws will find some place warm, which would mean away from the mountains, and my job would be easy. I just happened to stumble onto the horse thieves and I didn't think you'd be wantin' to sell that many horses, what with winter comin' on and such, so..." he shrugged and took another bite of the treat.

"And Esteban told me you had a woman with you

and she acted like she was your deputy, what's that all about?"

Cord chuckled, explained about Emaline and her family, and his plan of taking her to the stage, but that she was dragging her feet a little. "So, I'm not sure what to do with her. She was taken in by Lottie up at the stage station, but that would only be temporary."

"The way Esteban talked, he thought the two of you were together, you know..." he asked.

"Well, she has kinda grown on me, and to be truthful about it, she saved my bacon a couple times. First with the one they called Bull, he was about to choke me to death and she conked him with a big chair, broke the chair and Bull's head! Then after that, when we caught up with Miguel and he and Elivé thought they should shoot it out with us, she sided me and dropped Elivé with two shots. Then when the cougar had attacked your horses, she shot it down and well...she's been better than any deputy I could've had!"

"Sounds a mite dangerous too! She good lookin'?" asked Dawson, grinning.

Cord chuckled, smiled, "You betcha!" he mumbled.

"Well, you know," and he looked around the interior of the home, motioning to the other rooms and the furnishings, "this place needs a good couple to live here. And I need somebody to take it over!" He looked at Cord, waiting for his response.

Cord frowned, "But I thought you were going to use it as a second home?"

"No, I don't think so. My original plan was for Miguel and his woman to live here and manage it for me, but..." he shrugged. He painted his face with a concerned expression, "You had mentioned that you wanted to have a ranch someday, why not now?"

"I can't afford to buy a ranch, especially one like this!" declared Cord. "But, this would be my dream home, that's for certain sure."

"Then here's what I will do..." began Dawson and began to lay out the details for Cord to become the manager, operate the ranch and build the herds as well as market the cattle and horses. "And if you do as well as I think you will, this," he said, waving his arms around to indicate not just the home, but the entirety of the ranch, "could all be yours in, oh, about five years. What do you think?"

"Mr. Dawson, that is very generous, and it would be a dream come true, but..."

"Oh, don't worry. You'll earn it. I'm not giving you a gift, just an opportunity. And I know what it is to build a ranch and herds and workers and more. You will definitely earn it, but I think you're the man for the job," he explained as he leaned forward on the edge of his seat and reached for another empanada.

"That's a lot to think about. Could I have a few days? I need to talk to Marshal Shaffenburg, maybe talk to Em, but mostly, I'd like to pray about it."

Dawson let a slow smile split his face, "That's

what I like to hear. That just confirms what I thought about you and your good judgment. You do that, you take a week or two and be sure to let me know. My wife will be anxious for me to get back to Santa Fe and I'm thinkin' it'd be a bit warmer down there, so..." he shrugged.

The two men stood, shook hands, and Cord walked from the house. He made a quick look around and gave a thorough visual survey of the grounds and structures as he tightened the girth on the saddle. He swung aboard, looked around again, then with his heels in Kwitcher's ribs, the three friends, Kwitcher, Blue, and Cord, started back north.

32

PLANS

Cord was surprised to see the hubbub of activity around what appeared to be the construction of a pair of commercial buildings, side-by-side in the middle of nowhere. He had seen the activity when they came through with the horses but did not have the time to stop. The layout of the land was south of the river where a rocky butte stood as a sentinel to the mouth of the canyon of the Rio Grande, and on the flats below the foothills that lay in the shadows of the edge of the San Juan mountains. It was a logical place for a town, and with the many ranches, farms and other settlements, it seemed a likely location for a town. And with the rumblings of a gold rush come springtime, this would be a good place for supplies for the many prospectors that would be climbing the hills in every direction. Cord reined up and asked one of the workers, “So, whatchu buildin’?”

The man stopped, looked up at Cord and pointing to the two structures said, “That first’uns gonna be a general store, and prob’ly a bar, that second one’s gonna have a hotel and café. And on down thataway there’s gonna be a livery. Whole town, nearabouts! Now...gotta get busy ‘fore we get too much snow!” he said with a grin and he started to leave.

“What they gonna call it?” called out Cord.

“Well, I heard somebody say this used to be called Rio Del Norte, river of the north, and some were sayin’ it oughta just be Del Norte.” The man shrugged, started walking away with a wave over his shoulder.

Cord just chuckled, nudged Kwitcher back on the trail up river. The easy gait of Kwitcher on the familiar trail was enough for the many thoughts in Cord’s mind to chase one another about between memories and dreams. Many of the dreams had been shared with those that were special to Cord at the time. He thought of Yellow Singing Bird, the young Caputa Ute woman captive of the Comanche people, whom he had freed and brought back to her people. She had chosen to stay with Cord until her life was taken in a confrontation with outlaws, but they had spent many times together, sharing thoughts and dreams.

And the young woman, Tabitha Townsend, who would later become his wife, who helped him shape many of his dreams as they shared every moment of their lives. But her early death in the throes of childbirth ended several of those dreams before they were realized. And Lone Eagle, the woman shaman of the Uncompahgre Ute. They had talked often and shared hopes and dreams, but those would not be realized because of the demands of her position as shaman of the people and his position as marshal.

He had begun to think he was destined to spend the rest of his life alone, and then this rag-tailed wildcat called Emaline came into his life. He chuckled at the thought and the first meeting with Em when she introduced herself by way of crashing a bar chair over the head of Bull, the monster outlaw that was trying to choke the life out of Cord. And the way she helped out by shooting the second of the horse thieves when they met up with the stolen horse herd. She had implied afterward she was going to have to stay by his side just to keep him alive. He had been thinking about her a lot, both about what to do with her to get her on a stage back to her family in Kentucky or Missouri or wherever, and about how to keep her around because he was getting accustomed to her presence and her nearness and she had said she wasn't too sure about going back east, not really knowing anyone. He shook his head, chuckling to himself as he glanced about, looking for a likely place for a camp for the night.

The distance from the ranch to the stage stop was only a day's ride but Cord had spent part of the day getting the horses back to the ranch, and with a late start, the sun was already beginning to drop behind the mountains and dusk was crawling out from the shadows. He rounded the point of a small butte and entered a thicket of cottonwood and willows that sided the west branch of Piños Creek. Spotting a bit of a clearing with grass and close to the water, he nudged Kwitcher to the spot and stepped down to begin making his camp.

He stripped the gear from big grulla and picketed him within reach of water. Blue had already taken off on his usual exploratory tour of the area and Cord began building his campfire. He had a hankering for some trout for his supper and went to the creek, looking for a likely hole that he might find a trout or two and at a slight bend, he spotted a likely looking bank with a grassy flat that rolled over the edge to the water, just the kind of place where the big trout liked to hang out under the overhang.

With a glance about, Cord moved closer, bellied down and rolled up his sleeve. He slowly reached into the water, moved his hand in the cold and stretched easily under the edge of the embankment. With his palm open, he carefully moved his hand around, slowly getting the feel of the undercut. Cord felt the slow movement of a big trout and stealthily brought his palm up, his fingers outstretched and moved up to just behind the gills, then with a swift grab, he brought the trout out. He tossed it over his back onto the grass and watched as it flopped about. He waited just a moment and went for another one. Quickly grabbing another, he tossed it over to join the first but was startled by a voice that said, "Wow! How'd you do that?"

Cord quickly rolled to his back, his hand grabbing for his Colt but he stopped as he saw a boy of about nine or ten that was down on his knees, trying to catch up the flopping trout. Cord grinned, sat up and said, "Where'd you come from?"

The redheaded, freckle-faced boy sat up and faced Cord, "We got us a cabin o'er yonder." He nodded behind him toward the bigger butte that lay beyond the creek.

"Well, what're you doin' out this late? Shouldn't you be home with your ma and pa?" asked Cord, scowling at the boy who was still trying to grab the flopping fish.

"Ain't got no Pa, just me'n Ma and Sissy. Pa got kilt a while back an' now Ma says I'm the man o' the fam'ly." He made his declaration just as he finally grabbed the first and biggest fish.

"You wantin' that for supper?" asked Cord, nodding to the fish in his hands.

"Sure! Can I?" asked the grinning boy. "We ain't had fish in a long time!"

"So, what'chu been eatin'?" asked Cord, looking at the boy from under his brow, wondering about the boy and his family.

"Oh, whatever I can come up with which ain't much, lately."

"You got a knife you can clean that fish with?" asked Cord.

"Yeah! I can clean it!" he declared as he started digging in his pocket for his jackknife.

Cord rolled over on his stomach and returned to his hand fishing, wondering about the boy and his family. After bringing out four more fish, Cord rolled over and helped the boy with the cleaning. He showed him how to use a forked branch to slip through the gills of the fish and carry them all, then asked, "Your mom a good cook?"

The boy smiled broadly, "She's the *best* cook! Yessir!"

"Well, since I provided the fish, ya think she'd let me set down to supper with you?"

"We ain't got much, but she always says, *It's nice to share, Jody!*"

AND THE BOY had not stretched the truth at all. When Cord arrived, he was greeted by a smiling redhead with a miniature double clinging to her skirts. Jody introduced his mother, "Ma, this is Marshal Cordell Beckett, and Cord, this is Ma!"

She laughed and clarified, "My name is Naomi, Naomi MacGregor, and my shadow here is Maisie. Welcome to our home, Marshal. Please, come in and have a seat. And I'll get busy with the fish! They will be a welcome change, indeed. Thank you!"

"Could you use some bacon and flour, maybe

some coffee?" asked Cord, "I've got plenty and will be resupplying soon, so..." he shrugged.

"Well, the bacon could be used with the fish, and the flour could make biscuits, and I'm sure you would like some coffee, so...sure, that'd be very nice!"

And it was a fine meal, the best Cord had enjoyed for some time. During their conversation, Cord learned she had been a widow for a couple years, her husband had brought them west because of his dream of striking it rich in the gold fields, but he had lost his life to some claim jumpers. They had struggled ever since and she had no one to turn to for help but they were making it day to day. "And Jody there has become the man of the family and a pretty good hunter, but he really hasn't done too well as a fisherman, so, this fish was a welcome change," she laughed as she began clearing the table. "And how long have you been a marshal?" she asked.

Their conversation continued over coffee, but Cord, after his long day, was tired and determined to turn in, making his bed in the lean-to at the edge of the corral where Kwitcher and the rawboned horse of the boy hung their heads. Naomi had invited him to join them for breakfast, but he declined, explaining he would be well on his way before first light, but he left her the rest of the supplies he had in his saddlebags and with a grin, he surreptitiously put a twenty-dollar gold piece under the slab of bacon.

As he lay in his blankets, he was wondering how else he could help them and he had the idea that maybe if he got the ranch, she could do the cooking and housekeeping that the Mexican women were doing, because Dawson had said they would be returning to Santa Fe with him. Then he thought of Em and wondered just what she would think about being a rancher's wife with a housekeeper and cook. He chuckled at the thought of *wife* and rolled over to get some sleep.

33

CHANGES

THE COLD OF THE EARLY WINTER MORNING NIPPED AT Cord's ears and fingers as he swung aboard Kwitcher. The sun was just beginning to blush the morning sky with shades of pink, splashing some of the color on the bellies of the few clouds that lingered above the eastern mountains and the hint of color touched Cord's back as he rode from the cabin of the family.

The trail kept to the south side of the Rio Grande and wound among the different settlers. Some showed a lot of hard work with a good home, outbuildings, and fields that had yielded crops. Others were nothing more than a rough cabin or even a lean-to, some were dugouts, half buried in the adobe soil and with sod roofs, making them easily missed as he passed. There were a couple places that had the makings of a good ranch, just enough pastureland to support enough cattle for a family's livelihood.

The sun climbed higher and warmed Cord's back as he dozed in the saddle with the gentle rocking of Kwitcher, but when the big grulla stopped suddenly, Cord was brought awake and aware. The bleating of a sizable flock of sheep that blocked the trail made Kwitcher balk and start backstepping, but Cord used a taut rein and a stroke of the stallion's neck and an easy word to reassure the horse that it was alright. Two dogs were controlling the sizable flock and one shepherd followed closely behind. Cord continued to stroke and talk to Kwitcher as the sheep moved closer. Kwitcher stretched out his nose and sniffed at the woolly strangers, but he was not anxious to make friends.

As the flock passed, the shepherd lifted his crook, and waved at Cord, calling out, "Vaya Con Dios Señor!"

Cord waved and nodded in response and watched as they continued down the trail.

It was just past high noon when Cord rode into the yard of the stage station and was greeted by an apron-clad Emaline, smiling ear to ear. "Well, been wonderin' if you was comin' back for me!"

"Oh, I thought about just leavin' you here, but I had to come back for muh mule too!" Cord chuckled as he swung to the ground.

Em was wringing a wet rag she had been using to clean some tables, and at that remark threw it at Cord, scoring a hit on his chest, but he caught it and threw it back to the laughter of both. He stepped a little closer and asked, "Other'n throwin' things at me, didja miss me?" he chuckled.

"'Bout like I'd miss a headache!" she grumbled, but she was smiling broadly.

"So, you think I'm a headache, do ya?"

"I din't say that, but yes, I missed ya!" she fussed as he reached his hands to her waist to pull her close.

He was grinning as he looked down at her and said, "I been thinking. It might not be such a good idea to send you back east seein' as how you don't hardly know those folks and they might not be able to put up with a wildcat that hits people with chairs, shoots 'em, and such. I was thinkin' you might need a little more tamin'."

"Tamin'? And what makes you think you could do that?" asked Em, smiling up at Cord.

"Oh, I know it wouldn't be easy, but if I kept you purty close, you know, always within reach and such, and if you got to misbehavin' and needed a good spankin' and such, well, I could do that!" he laughed.

"You just try it, buster!" growled Em, doing her best not to smile or laugh.

"Hey there, young lady! I ain't payin' you to entertain the men! You got work to do!" declared Lottie as she came to the open door.

"Payin'? You ain't payin' me!" answered Em as she turned to face the grinning Lottie.

The older woman stepped around Em and extended her hand, "Glad to see you back Cord. She was gettin' to be a handful—always goin' to the window to look down the road to see if you was comin' back, askin' questions 'bout everything havin' to do with keepin' house, cookin' and such, my oh my!" she smiled and laughed. "A body'd think you had been gone a couple weeks instead of a couple days!"

Cord chuckled, letting Em go as he looked at Lottie and asked, "Where's Zed? I'd like to talk to him about somethin'?"

"Oh, he had to take some horses up the trail a bit. They're puttin' in another station and needed the relief horses, but he'll be back for supper. Put'chur horse in the barn and come on in for some coffee and such!"

"I'll do that," answered Cord with a glance to Em and a nod to Lottie.

THE CONVERSATION at the supper table was centered on the proposed purchase of the ranch. There had been no stage during the day and it was just the four that were involved. It wasn't so much that Zed or Lottie knew anything about ranching, but sometimes it just helps to talk about a situation or opportunity to get it out in the open and look at every possibility and more. When Cord finished explaining the proposition of John Dawson and the ranch, the others sat quiet for a moment until Lottie asked, "Are you going to give up being a marshal then?"

"Yes, ma'am, it might not be immediately, but as soon as Marshal Shaffenburg can get a replacement."

"And you'n Em would be together in this deal?" asked Zed, glancing from one to the other.

Cord grinned, glanced to Em who sat to his right and had a question on her face, and answered, "Reckon so...the ways things have been, she's been protectin' me and I prob'ly couldn't live long enough to pay for the ranch without her by my side." He reached for her hand, and she readily clasped hands with him, grinning broadly and her eyes dancing with happiness.

"Then I think it's something you can't pass up!" declared Lottie.

"It's definitely quite an opportunity—one that only comes once in a lifetime," added Zed. "It'll be a lot of work, but you can build yourselves a life there."

THEY WALKED hand-in-hand from the station to the corral with the big moon smiling down on them and Blue beside them. Cord looked down at her, her face bright in the moonlight, and said, "I know I should have talked to you about it all first, but..." he shrugged, "I hadn't really given a lot of thought about how I felt about you until we were apart, and it just seemed like that's the way it oughta be."

Em smiled as she looked up at him and said, "I know. I felt the same when I watched you ride away. I couldn't stand the thought that you might not come back, and then the idea of you sendin' me away to go back east and..." she shook her head, looked down and back up at him, and said, "You've made me very happy. I just couldn't think of not being with you. So...tell me more about this ranch!"

The rattle of trace chains and the rumble of wheels on the rocky trail brought their attention to the trail and the arrival of a stagecoach. Zed motioned to Cord for some help and Cord waved, turned to Em and said, "I'm gonna help Zed. You might be some help to Lottie, if you want."

"I will, we'll talk later..." she said and smiled as he left to help Zed.

Although the stage came in with a four-up team, they would need a six-up from here as they headed deeper into the mountains. It was a long and steady climb, and the roads were yet to be improved for easy travel. Cord set about catching and harnessing the new team while Zed unhooked and dropped the harness of the tired team.

As he worked, the driver leaned on the fence rail and asked, "You're new, ain't cha?"

Cord chuckled, "No, I'm just passin' through and helpin' Zed. Since your schedule is a little unpredictable..." Cord shrugged as he worked on the harness.

"Oh, don't I know it! But it's gettin' better. They got stage stations set up new most every run. Got a new one down to Del Norte, what used to be La Loma, and another'n o'er to La Garita. Makes things better when we don't have to go so far with tired horses. Make better time too!"

"You say they have a station at Del Norte?"

"Ummhmm, first stop was this mornin'."

"In town?"

"At the livery...just got a corral and a lean-to for now, but they're buildin' 'em a barn and such."

"You don't say," chuckled Cord. "I'm thinkin' 'bout settlin' in Del Norte. You know, get married, settle down, raise horses an' kids..." He grinned at the thought.

"Got'chu a woman?"

"Yup! She just walked into the station there, helpin' Lottie with your passengers and the meal."

"Married?"

"Not yet, but soon's we find us a preacher, we'll get it done."

"What's it worth to you?"

"What'chu mean?" asked Cord, layin' his arm across the big lead of the team and scowling at the driver. He saw the man was grinning as he stuffed some tobacco in his lip.

"Got me a preacher on the coach! Says he's a friend o' preacher Dyer, you know, the preacher that delivers mail on snowshoes!"

Cord frowned at the man, remembering Pastor Dyer, the man who did the ceremony when he and Tabby were married. They had been friends for several years. Cord led the team out of the corral, handed them off to Zed and followed the driver into the station. They stepped up to the table, the driver seating himself and he nodded to the man opposite, "Pastor, this here fella says he's lookin' for a preacher!"

The young man looked up from his meal, smiled, and said, "How may I help you, sir?"

Cord noticed everyone at the table and the women, Lottie and Emaline, by the stove, all stopped and looked up at that statement, glancing from Cord to the preacher.

Cord put his leg over the bench and seated himself across from the man and asked, "He said you were friends with Pastor Dyer, that right?"

"Why, yes. Pastor Dyer is my friend and mentor. He helped me and taught me a lot. We've worked together also. Pastor Dyer was going to Breckenridge, wants to start and build a church there. I'm going through this part of the country, letting the Lord lead as to where I might do the same. How do you know Pastor Dyer?"

"Oh, I met him a few years back, up at Fairplay, Oro City, and thereabouts. He's the man that married me'n my wife."

"Oh, that's good. And what did you need my services for?"

"Oh, thinkin' 'bout gettin' married. Need somebody to do the service."

The young man frowned, “Most folks think one wife is enough. Are you Mormon?”

Cord grinned, dropped his eyes and slowly shook his head, “No, I’m not Mormon. I’m Christian and happy for it. And my first wife died, but now the Lord has brought another woman into my life and we believe it is His will that we get married and start a new life together.” He glanced over to a smiling and slightly embarrassed Ema who dropped her eyes and fidgeted about as Lottie reached her arm around her shoulders and hugged her.

The parson looked at the driver, “Will we have time for a short ceremony?”

The driver chuckled, “Depends on the meal…” he looked at Lottie and Em, “Got’ny dessert?”

“I NOW PRONOUNCE you man and wife. May the Lord richly bless you and keep you all the days of your life together!” declared the young parson, smiling broadly and added, “You may now kiss the bride!” He watched, grinning, as Cord and Em sealed their vows with a kiss and the applause of the rest of the passengers and Zed and Lottie.

Lottie gave Em a big hug, looked at Cord and said, “You two can sleep in the loft tonight, there’s lots of warm hay up there!” she giggled and glanced to a mischievous smiling Zed, who nodded his agreement.

It was late afternoon when the newlyweds rode through the site of Del Norte. The buildings were going up faster than Cord thought possible and more people had arrived, pitching tents and starting work on lean-tos and cabins in anticipation of the coming winter, all hopeful of being among the first to take to the mountains come spring. They rode through the ruckus, and as they neared the ranch, Cord reined up on a slight rise that offered a good view and began pointing out the different features and more of the ranch. Em was surprised and amazed and looked at Cord and said, "And that's going to be our home?"

"It is."

"And the MacGregor family will join us, Naomi and the kids?"

"They will. They said they'd be here tomorrow and help us get settled. She anxious to be a help, cleanin' an' cookin' and such, and her son, well, he wants to be a real cowboy!"

Em looked at Cord and smiled broadly, "It's more than a dream come true, it's an answer to prayer!"

Cord grinned, nodded, and nudged Kwitcher to get a move on, waved Blue to take the lead and Cord felt the lead line of the mule pull taut and with a smile to his bride said, "Let's go home!"

A LOOK AT:

THE COVENANT

From the bestselling author of The Plainsman Western series comes a 2024 Independent Press Award Distinguished Favorite for Historical Fiction—an exciting and explosive new Western series.

It is a time of uncertainty in the infancy of a growing nation. The Wild West is open and beckoning to displaced men and families, many of whom choose to travel to the unsettled frontier, dreaming of new homes, land, and even riches. But few reckon on those who have lived in those lands for centuries—the native peoples. Blackfoot, Crow, Sioux, and more.

Elijah McCain, fresh from the Union army where he attained the rank of Lieutenant Colonel with the Mounted Rifles—a cavalry unit under General Sherman—has returned home to find his wife on her deathbed, pleading for her twin sons. She elicits a promise, a covenant, from her husband: "Find our boys, and bring them home."

So, Eli vows to do just that. Holding her hand as she slips from life, he promises to bring their sons home—no matter what. Even if it's the undoing of dreams, lives, and more.

AVAILABLE NOW

ABOUT THE AUTHOR

Born and raised in Colorado into a family of ranchers and cowboys, B.N. Rundell is the youngest of seven sons. Juggling bull riding, skiing, and high school, graduation was a launching pad for a hitch in the Army Paratroopers. After the army, he finished his college education in Springfield, MO, and together with his wife and growing family, entered the ministry as a Baptist preacher.

With many years as a successful pastor and educator, he retired from the ministry and followed in the footsteps of his entrepreneurial father and started a successful insurance agency, which is now in the hands of his trusted nephew. Having finally realized his life-long dream, B.N. has turned his efforts to writing a variety of books, from children's picture books and young adult adventure books, to the historical fiction and Western genres, which are his first loves.

www.ingramcontent.com/pod-product-compliance
Lightning Source LLC
LaVergne TN
LVHW040216110826
845146LV00005B/1313

* 9 7 9 8 8 9 5 6 7 5 8 3 0 *